Hustle

DISCREET EDITION

www.chellebliss.com

CHELLE BLISS

USA TODAY BESTSELLING AUTHOR

MEN OF INKED: SOUTHSIDE SERIES

Join the Chicago Gallo Family with their strong alphas, sassy women, and tons of fun.

Book 1 - Maneuver (Lucio)
Book 2 - Flow (Daphne)
Book 3 - Hook (Angelo)
Book 4 - Hustle (Vinnie)
Book 5 - Love (Angelo)

Maneuver   Flow   Hook   Hustle   Love
CHELLE BLISS   CHELLE BLISS   CHELLE BLISS   CHELLE BLISS   CHELLE BLISS

HUSTLE COPYRIGHT

Published by Bliss Ink & Chelle Bliss
Published on March 26th 2019
Edited by Silently Correcting Your Grammar
Proofread by Julie Deaton & Rosa Sharon
Cover Design @ Chelle Bliss

To Aunt Debbie,

*Thank you for being you. No one could ask for a better aunt.
You're loving, fierce, and bake the best damn cookies, cake,
and pie.*

*But seriously… Thank you for everything you do. From
taking care of grandma and grandpa to just being there when
always.*

You're a selfless person. A rare gem.

I love you… Always.
Chelle

CHAPTER 1
VINNIE

"UGH. How long are you going to be?"

The voice comes from somewhere behind me.

"What's the problem?" I grunt into the cardboard, trying not to drop everything as I step to the back of the elevator.

"I have to get upstairs," the woman says. "And you're hogging the elevator."

I jam the boxes in a corner, gritting my teeth and wishing I had hired movers to help with this bullshit. Who knew I had so much stuff? Between my place in Indiana and my old bedroom above the bar, I had amassed more shit than I knew what to do with. But this chick, the one tapping her foot against the cold marble in the lobby doesn't give a crap about any of that.

When I bought the unit, I didn't think about the fact that there was only one elevator for the entire fifty-unit building. I was too excited about buying my first place, which was also the only available penthouse on the block.

"I'll make a spot for you." I back out of the half-empty elevator, pushing boxes aside for the woman.

She groans, bumping into my shoulder as she walks by me. "Inconsiderate," she mumbles.

She may be bitchy, but the calves on her could choke me out if she wrapped them the right way around my neck.

Then there's that ass. High and tight in running shorts and a half tank, showing off her black tramp stamp like a beacon, calling out to my cock, just above her waistband.

When she spins around, her front is more spectacular than the view from the back. Big tits, skin the color of caramel frosting, and long brown hair dancing over her breasts just like my hands would if given half the chance.

"Are you done yet?" She crosses her arms over her chest.

She's caught me looking, but hell if I'm going to admit it. "With what?"

How could I not stare? There's no way she walks around in that outfit and doesn't expect to catch an eye or two. She might as well be naked between the amount of skin she's showing and the tightness of the clothes she's wearing.

She moves one hand to her face, and my eyes follow. "My eyes are up here."

I nearly swallow my tongue as I take in her full pink lips, high cheekbones, and bronze-colored eyes.

She's just a hot chick, Vinnie.

I'd been with dozens of hot girls, but damn it, I'm a connoisseur of fine women. One is more beautiful than the next.

I don't use them either. I worship their beauty and softness, losing myself in the pleasure I give to them as well as myself.

"Are you done gawking?"

I can't take my eyes off her mouth as she speaks. The way the corner of her lips turns up a little as they move is hot as hell.

It's like I've gone stupid, which is something new for me.

Maybe it's the fact that I haven't gotten laid in weeks, deciding it was better to keep my junk in my pants as I transition from college into my new life as a professional football player and step into adulthood.

I clear my throat and grab more boxes. "I wasn't gawking."

She drops a shoulder and tilts her head, totally calling me on my bullshit. "You were staring."

"I was trying to figure out if I could fit more boxes on before we head up," I lie through my goddamn teeth.

There's no way I'm giving this girl, who's throwing attitude like it's her job, any more ammunition to toss in my face than she already has.

I set another stack of boxes just inside the doors, and

as I stand, I can't help but let my eyes linger a little too long on her legs.

"You're doing it again," she tells me, and that damn foot starts tapping once more.

I straighten and shake off the wicked voodoo this chick has put on me, deciding to turn on the charm that's gotten me into all the ladies' panties since I was fifteen. "I'm Vinnie Gallo." I put my hand between us with the killer smile that's scored me so much pussy, even Hugh Hefner would be jealous.

She looks down but doesn't even try to touch me. "Bianca Hernandez."

"Bianca." I like the way her name rolls off my tongue. I don't think I've ever had a Bianca in my bed. "I'm moving into 11A." I pull my hand back as I slide into the elevator in the small space between Bianca and the keypad. We're so close, I can smell the sweet scent of the perfume she sprayed on her skin this morning.

"Great." There's no joy in her voice. She hasn't bothered to look at me again, finding the brown carpeting under our feet far more interesting than me. "I'm in 11B."

I smile wider. "We're neighbors."

I hadn't even bothered to ask the real estate agent about the people inside the building or who would be next to me with the entire floor to ourselves. I'll barely be home anyway and didn't think it would matter. But...this is a very interesting turn of events.

"I've never been so happy in my life," she says sarcastically.

I shouldn't like this crabby chick with an attitude bigger than my sister's, but there's something about her that makes me want to peel away the layers and see what's underneath.

"Want to hit eleven? I'm late and don't have all day to chitchat."

"Sorry." I punch the button for the eleventh floor and glance her way. "Busy day, huh?"

She slowly turns her face upward, gazing at me with those honey eyes. "Since we're going to be alone on the eleventh floor, let's get a few things straight."

I nod but keep my mouth shut, because my mother and sister taught me when to listen and when to speak. This is clearly a moment to listen to the sassy little Bianca.

"I get up early, so I don't have late-night parties or put up with rowdy, loud assholes keeping me up. I work from home, and I like the peace and serenity living on the eleventh floor provides me. Don't ruin it."

"Noted," I say as she gawks at my arms.

I flex a little because my muscles are no doubt impressive. I spend more than half my daily workout on my arms, trying to make them stronger than ever before to earn the starting spot on the field this season.

"Do not think we're going to be buddy-buddy just because we share a few walls." Her gaze lingers on my forearms, much like mine did on her calves.

"What if I run out of sugar?"

"There's a corner store down the street," she says quickly.

"Cream?"

"I use soy milk."

Damn.

The girl has all her bases covered like I'm not the first asshole to have impure thoughts about her, which I'm totally sure I'm not. The attitude probably chases everyone away, but I'm used to attitude. Growing up Gallo, it came with the territory.

If anything, the way she's trying to keep me at a distance, presenting herself as a challenge, just makes me want to try a little more.

The elevator lurches, and Bianca falls forward into my arms. It's like a sign from above, and I know the big guy is on my side. "I got you." I grab on to her waist, steadying her, but also keeping her close because she feels good against me.

Her tiny hands wrap around my biceps as she pushes herself backward and glares up at me with narrowed eyes. "What are you doing?" Her fingernails bite into my skin, mixing a little pain with the pleasure of her body pressed against mine.

I instantly release her waist. "I didn't want you to fall."

"I'm fine. This happens all the time," she says, but she hasn't bothered to take her hands off me. Her smooth palms are still flat against my skin, almost groping my muscles like a cat does a fluffy blanket when it's happy.

When I glance down, looking at where our bodies

are still connected, she finally pulls away. "Sorry." She clears her throat.

"Don't be," I tell her because I'm not sorry in the slightest. I want to see those slender fingers with cherry-red polish wrapped around my cock as those plump pink lips suck me off. "Shit happens."

By the way she's staring at me, I think she's going to kiss me, moving in for the kill. I hold my breath, feeling my skin tingle all over at the excitement of the moment.

Fucking in an elevator is an experience, one I've already had and would happily replicate with this hot little firecracker. But she doesn't kiss me. She doesn't touch me. She pushes the button on the wall behind me, and the elevator starts to move again.

We stare at each other without speaking for the last few floors. Maybe she feels the same crackle in the thick air. How could she not? I felt it the moment her skin touched mine. The second she fell into my arms like she was always meant to be there.

She practically runs out of the elevator as soon as it comes to a stop, sliding between the doors before they've fully opened.

"It was nice meeting you, Bianca," I call out, watching her ass shake as she stalks toward her end of the hallway.

She jams her key into the lock and finally looks at me again. "Let's not make a habit of this," she says before her eyes rake over my body.

"Fuck," I groan while I adjust my semihard cock in

my sweat pants as she disappears inside her place. "Do not fuck the neighbor," I tell myself.

This isn't college or a rental. The last thing I need is to get my fill of the hot Latina princess and then have to see her pouty lips every day, taunting me as she fantasizes about killing me because I did her wrong.

I have a problem.

I'm a lover of women.

All kinds of women.

Typically, not the same woman more than once unless they have a special skill I just have to sample one more time.

Sleeping with Bianca wouldn't end well for either of us.

I kick open the door to my penthouse, stopping in the foyer to take in the sweeping view of the city and the stadium where I'll play for the next year.

I'm home.

Back in my old stomping grounds with a hometown crowd ready to cheer my name. I should be thinking about the endless hours of unpacking I have ahead of me, but as I wander toward the floor-to-ceiling windows, all I can think about is the raging hard-on I now have courtesy of the sexy little number on the other side of the wall.

Fucking perfect.

CHAPTER 2
VINNIE

"WELL, YOU DONE FUCKED UP." Clarence runs a towel over his wet hair, giving me that judgmental look only he can pull off. "For a city kid, you sure are a dumb mothafucka."

"Dude, I didn't do anything." I lean over, resting my elbows on my knees, and stare at the puddle of water near my feet. "Why can't she like someone else?"

For the first time in my life, I don't want the attention of a woman. Tracie Turner is the team owner's granddaughter—and very much batshit crazy.

Before I signed with Chicago, she followed me around and would show up at campus parties, even though she wasn't a student, and did everything she could to get my attention and my cock.

Nothing worked.

I have very few limits, but crazy-as-shit is on top of my "*Do Not Fuck*" list.

I was at least that smart. I could do mildly wacky,

but Tracie was way beyond that point. She was one step away from a padded cell and a straightjacket, but her family's money sheltered her, keeping her safe and walking the streets.

I thought she'd leave me alone once I started training for the start of the season. I had hoped someone in her family or the front office would tell her to back off, but no one did. Or if they had, she didn't listen.

Clarence shakes his head as he drops his towel to the tile floor of the locker room. "You're too nice to that insane bitch."

"I try to be nice to everyone. Hello," I say, pointing at my chest with my thumbs. "I'm the new kid, dumbass. I can't be a total dick."

I haven't proven myself on the field or earned a starting spot, something I've dreamed of since I was a little boy. With the retirement of the previous quarterback, the spot is open, but there are three of us fighting for the position.

I won't do anything to ruin my chances, including being mean to Tracie.

"To her, you can."

I scrub my hand across my face, wishing I could find a way to pass Tracie on to someone else. "There has to be a way to get rid of her."

"You just have to wait her out. She'll eventually find someone else to harass, but that won't be until winter when the new meat hits the scene." He laughs, finding joy in my agony. "For now, you're stuck with her following you around, trying to get in your pants." He yanks his shirt over his head before leveling me with his dark-brown eyes. "Do not, under any circumstances, sleep with her."

My mouth gapes open. "Come on. Give me some credit, Clarence."

He raises an eyebrow. "I've seen better men than you fall victim to her brand of insanity. They were immediately traded and eventually faded out of existence."

"Fuck," I hiss, standing quickly to finish dressing and get the hell out of the locker room.

"Tracie," someone calls out from the other side of the lockers, alerting the entire room that the nutty bitch has arrived. "You're not supposed to be in here."

Clarence looks at me and winces. "You better hustle your ass right out of here." He pauses for a minute and looks around the locker room. "Better yet, don't leave until she does. Stay in a public place surrounded by lots of people. Don't let her get you alone."

"Will you stay with me?" I ask him, hoping he'll at least be by my side as I try to stop Tracie from touching me.

He shakes his head. "I got a hot date with my lady, and if I'm late, there will be hell to pay."

"Way to have my back, bro."

"Sweetheart, there you are," Tracie says as she comes around the lockers and finds us staring at each other, not moving.

Clarence doesn't even try to hide his laughter as

Tracie's high heels click on the tile behind me. He doesn't bother with a hello or a goodbye before he walks away, leaving me alone with her. Well, as alone as one can be in a locker room filled with people, including the press.

"Hey." I don't look in her direction as I reach into my locker for my shirt.

The last thing I want to do is be half dressed around her. She's always trying to touch me, and the way she looks at my bare chest always gives me the creeps. I'm not sure if she wants to lick me or peel off my skin with a small Swiss Army knife and wear it around like the insane fucker in *Silence of the Lambs*.

She leans against the lockers, raking her eyes across my skin before I can pull the shirt over my head. "There's a hot party tonight."

"You have fun." I tuck the hem of the shirt into my pants, making it impossible for her to reach underneath and scrape her pointy fingernails across my abs.

"I need a date," she says like I should care. "And guess who's taking me?"

"Marty?" I shrug and play stupid. There's no way in hell I'm being her date for anything.

"You, silly." She giggles and my skin crawls.

"I can't. I have to work at the bar tonight."

"Oh." She raises her eyebrows, and a smile spreads across her face. "I can hang out there instead."

I immediately regret letting that information slip and have to backtrack. "Go to the party. You deserve a fun night."

She reaches out to touch my forearm, but I back away. "I gotta run. I'm late."

Tracie's eyes narrow as she pulls her arm back against her chest like she's been burned. "Maybe I'll see you tonight."

"Sure. Sure." I nod, but I already want to call some buddies to work the door at the bar, banning her from walking inside and causing a scene again.

The last time Tracie showed up at Hook & Hustle, I almost had to carry her out of the place. She scared away practically every female customer in the place, stating they were being a little too flirtatious with me. She went as far as to announce to the room that I was her man and strictly off-limits. I'm still catching shit for her little stunt, and it was two months ago.

I start to walk away when she says, "Don't forget who you belong to."

I feel my entire body stiffen at her words, and I spin around to face her with no amusement on my face. "Tracie..." I lower my voice and deepen my tone. I don't want the other people in the locker room to hear what I'm about to say to this woman. "Let's get something straight."

She crosses her arms and smirks as I stride in her direction. "What's that?"

I stop a few feet away, just out of touching distance. "I am not now, nor will I ever be, *yours*."

She pushes off the lockers, walking in my direction, looking at me like I'm prey. "You'd refuse me? You know who my granddaddy is, right?"

I stand my ground, crossing my arms over my chest and puffing out my body as big as possible like a wild animal. "I know exactly who your granddaddy is, Tracie, but that doesn't give you the right to lord that shit over my head. We are nothing. We always will be nothing. If you want to run off to your granddaddy with some lie about me—" I glance toward the locker room door "—then go right ahead and get it over with already."

She places a hand on my chest and pouts. "I thought we had something special, Vinnie."

"We don't," I say, driving the point home again because Tracie can't seem to fathom that I don't want anything she's offering.

"We had a moment."

"We had nothing, and anyway, I have a girlfriend. Imagine the scandal that would cause your family. Your granddaddy wouldn't be too happy."

She raises an eyebrow, digging her fingernails into my chest through my T-shirt. "Who?"

Like a dumbass, I blurt out the only chick who's been on my mind. "Bianca."

We passed each other in the lobby this morning, her coming back from her workout, all sweaty and hot, and me heading to the team's training facility. I said hello, but she just stared at the ground and grunted as she ran by me without so much as an upward glance.

"Bianca," Tracie repeats as if the name is acidic in her mouth.

"Yo, Gallo. Coach needs to see you," Tre, our best

tight end, says as he walks around the corner, seeing Tracie and me a little too close for anyone's comfort.

I give him a chin lift, wishing I could thank him for saving me in this moment. "On it," I call out without moving my eyes away from Tracie. "I have to go. We're done here. Either talk to your granddaddy, or get off my case. You're not going to blackmail me into sleeping with you, Tracie. Maybe it's time you find a new victim."

If looks could kill, I'd be a dead man.

———

"Gallo," the coach says as he rocks back in his high-back office chair, staring at me across his desk. "We're impressed with your ability on the field, and the guys on the team seem to like you, which isn't always the case."

I can feel a but coming somewhere in this conversation. I brace myself for the "But you don't have a hope or prayer to start this season," or "But we think you can do better."

"But we have an issue with you and Tracie."

The one thing I hadn't prepared myself for was for that to come out of the coach's mouth.

I furrow my eyebrows. "Me and Tracie? There's no me and Tracie. You know she's crazy, right?"

Normally, I wouldn't go around throwing out those kinds of terms, but there is no other way to describe her.

Coach rubs the back of his neck and sighs. "She's different."

If different is code for delusional, then he's pretty damn close.

"I have a girlfriend, Coach, and her name isn't Tracie." I keep piling on the lies, digging my grave deeper. "I keep telling Tracie to leave me alone, but she hasn't listened."

He leans forward and places his weathered hands on the desk. "I was afraid of this."

How could her grandfather possibly let her anywhere near the players on this team? Her behavior isn't normal. Her inability to face the truth, no matter how many times I tell her, makes her nuttier than a Snickers bar.

"I'll talk to Old Man Turner about his grand-daughter and see if I can get her barred for the season."

"He'd do that?"

"Listen." He rubs his hands together slowly, staring at me as he pauses for a moment. "The man has a lot of faith in you. He thinks you could be the one who brings the city back to the team and gets us to the play-offs in a few years. If he knows Tracie is bothering you, I'm sure he'll handle her."

I forget about Tracie for a minute and think about the other words he said. *Play-offs. You could be the one.* I like the sound of those words, and I know my spot is solid as long as I don't mess shit up with Tracie and her granddaddy.

"Steer clear of her until I can talk to him."

I pinch the bridge of my nose as I lean forward, resting my elbow on my knees. "I have been. The woman comes into the locker room and accosts me on the daily."

"Shower and prep at home until further notice. You live nearby, right?"

"Just down the street."

"Take no chances for a few days. Bring your girl-friend to the team party this weekend so people can see you with someone else in public. It'll help in putting distance between any whispers about you and Tracie."

"Shit," I mumble and take a deep breath before I relax back into the chair and try to think of a way to get Bianca to accompany me to the party. "I'll see if she's free."

"Make her free, Gallo. This is too important to fuck up. You hear me?"

"I hear you, Coach." I nod, but I know this isn't an easy task. I can't even get Bianca to look at me, let alone be my date for a night.

I have a feeling I'm going to have to grovel and pray she'll at least take enough pity on me to accompany me for a few hours to save face with Mr. Turner.

CHAPTER 3
BIANCA

"YOU'RE NOT GETTING ANY YOUNGER," my mother tells me through the speakerphone as I wash the final dish sitting in the sink. "George is a perfect match for you, and he can father many children for our family."

"Ma, seriously. Have you gone off the deep end?"

"I don't know what that means, but I am very serious. What's wrong with George?"

"How much time do you have?" I laugh, but she doesn't find my sense of humor very funny.

George is just as boring as his name. He's a computer programmer, spending just as many hours chained to a desk as me. He's socially awkward and has been ever since we were kids, probably due to the fact that he barely left his room because he was addicted to video games. He's not awful to look at, but damn, he's about as interesting as watching water boil.

"He has a good job, his family adores you, and he owns his own car."

For fuck's sake. I roll my eyes. "So, if a man owns a car, he's husband material?"

I don't know what century my mother is living in, but it's not this one. Most women don't need a man to make their life complete, and I'm one of them. I'm successful, with my own place and a car. I don't need a man to provide for me, but that doesn't stop her from trying.

"He has nice teeth too," she adds, like that little detail should be enough to seal the deal.

If this conversation goes on any longer, my eyes are going to be permanently lodged in the back of my eye sockets. "Do you even hear yourself?"

From the moment I turned twenty-five, my mother has been on my back about getting married and having children as quickly as possible. I keep hearing about the fact that, by my age, she had three children and had been married for five years. I get that was the norm for her generation, but I'm too focused on my career and unwilling to settle for any relationship that's less than spectacular.

But by her standards, I am failing at life. Soon, my eggs will shrivel up and die, leaving me barren and alone for the rest of my life.

"I want you to be happy, Bianca."

I take out my frustration on the dish towel, crumpling it into a tiny ball. "I am happy, Ma. I have a good job, a nice home, and my own car. I don't need a man."

"You do what you want, honey!" my dad yells in the background.

Somehow, my mother still buys into the old-world thinking. A woman is nothing without a man by her side. It doesn't matter how successful I am or how big my bank account is—in her eyes, I need a man. Thank God my father doesn't think that way.

"Thanks, Daddy." I smile, knowing my dad's always got my back.

"Be quiet," Ma tells him, and I'm pretty sure he's going to pay for his comment later.

"Hush now, Ana. Bianca's young. Let her live a little."

"Don't touch me," Ma says with a small laugh. "Your charms won't work on me."

I gag a little because I know what *charms* she's talking about. "I have to go. I'm late," I say because I don't want to listen to my father trying to woo my mom again.

"Late? It's seven. Where are you going at this hour?" my mother asks.

"I have a date." I stare down at my bare feet with their chipped toenail polish and leave out the most important information because she'll go off the rails.

"Oh. Then I'll let you run." The happiness in her voice is clear as day. "Call me tomorrow and tell me how it went."

"I will. I always do." I lie every time too.

Six months ago, I made a promise to myself.

Stay celibate for one year. Clear my head and my life

of all the assholes from my past. I've never had a good track record when it comes to men. I always seem to pick the biggest losers. Every single one of them has been a cheater, a liar, or a player.

I don't have time for any of that bullshit in my life. Their inability to be genuine and keep their dicks in their pants affected my work, and nothing will keep me from my goals.

I haven't told my mother I've been avoiding men for months, trying to keep my head clear to finish writing my current book. She'd go bananas if she knew; therefore, I lie to her because it's easier than explaining my reasoning to her.

"Wear the red dress," she says, still trying to run my life. "And bring him to the party because I'd hate for you to come alone."

"Bye, Ma." I tap the end button before she can say anything else. Sometimes, talking to my mother is like running a mental marathon. It's exhausting going over the same topics again and again.

I practically throw myself on the couch after I turn on the television, waiting for my streaming app to start. Over the winter, I started bingeing every television series I could get my hands on. It helped fill the nights and settle my mind after a long day typing away at the keyboard. Winter bled into summer, and I couldn't seem to find the energy to go out at night with my friends and hit the club scene. I was over nightlife and men, preferring my couch and television.

Richard, the hero and total hottie in my newest

obsession, is about to bed the woman he's been chasing for a year. I'm glued to the screen, holding my breath and waiting for the moment when their lips finally touch. I can feel the tension the closer their mouths are to each other's.

Knock. Knock.

I groan and drop my head. Even though I've watched two seasons in the last week, I feel like I've been waiting forever for them to kiss. Whoever is here, they'd better have a damn good reason for picking this moment to knock on my door.

Without thinking, I run to the door and swing it open like a woman possessed because, damn it, they're interrupting my favorite show.

I'm met with the greenest eyes belonging to my sexy new neighbor. The same guy I've been avoiding at all costs because he's so good-looking, I know he's nothing but trouble.

"Hey." He smirks.

The flush that crept up my chest the other day when I met him is now a full-on burn. The man is gorgeous. There's no denying that. I'm pretty sure, by the way he acts, he knows it too.

"Can I help you?"

"I'm Vinnie."

"I remember." I try to keep my eyes on his face, but it's almost impossible since he's shirtless. The man's body is unreal. He must spend endless hours in the gym, lifting and squatting, to sculpt his muscles to such perfection.

His focus dips, and mine follows to my workout bra and yoga pants. Although I'm dressed, I feel more naked than he actually is.

He reaches back, rubbing his neck. "I was wondering if you'd do me…"

I don't really know what he says next because I'm too busy watching the way his biceps flex as he runs his hand back and forth across his skin and thinking about how I'd very much like to do him.

The movement puts me in a trance. A sexless, I-haven't-been-fucked-in-six-months kind of rapture.

When I finally look at his face again, he's staring at me with that sexy I-know-you're-checking-me-out smirk.

I blink because I'm pretty sure my mind heard something completely different from what came out of his mouth. "Excuse me?"

"Would you do that favor for me? I'd owe you big-time. I'll repay you any way I can."

I push the hair that's fallen out of my messy bun away from my face, suddenly feeling like I'm standing in the desert with no shelter from the blazing sun. "What favor?"

He drops his hand to his side, and with the way he's standing and the overhead lighting of the hallway, he looks more like a statue created for some museum display of the perfect male form. "I know we got off on the wrong foot yesterday."

I cringe, knowing I was an asshole. "I'm sorry about

that. I was having a bad day and didn't mean to take it out on you."

"It's okay. I have those too sometimes."

He's sweet, which immediately puts me on edge because there's no way this hot-as-fuck guy could actually be nice.

"I know I'm reaching with asking you this, and you don't owe me anything, so feel free to tell me to fuck off, but my career may be on the line."

I grab on to the door handle, using it to keep me upright. Between the tension on the television and now the hotness at my door, my body feels more alive than it has in months. "What do you need again?"

I want to slap myself. Hard. He's been at my door for under a minute, and I already sound like the world's biggest idiot. I'm having trouble keeping up with the conversation, and I wonder what he's thinking about me.

His hand goes back to his neck, and my eyes fly to his muscle. I can do this. I can pay attention and not gawk at the way his skin moves like it's begging for me to reach out and run my fingers over the silky smoothness.

"I was wondering if you'd go out with me for a night. No strings attached."

My eyes snap to his face, but I'm at a loss for words as he continues.

"I'm in a jam at work and wanted to know if you'd accompany me to a business dinner. You'd be saving me big-time. I'll pay you back, of course."

I jerk my head back as what he's asking washes over me. "You want me to go on a date with you?"

"It's a very public party. I promise to be a complete gentleman and keep my hands to myself."

"Oh. Well, I..." I don't know what to say, actually. That was the last thing I expected to come out of his mouth.

Then it hits me. I can hear my mother's voice playing on repeat in my head, nagging me about finding myself a man. My parents' anniversary party is coming up, and the entire family will be there. If I show up alone, I'll never hear the end of how sad it is that little Bianca can't find herself a man.

We'll swap. It's a perfect idea. I'll do this favor for him and go to his work dinner, but he has to accompany me to the anniversary party.

"I'll tell you what," I say, but I can't believe the words are coming out of my mouth. "I'll go with you, but only if you go to a party with me."

His eyes light up, stealing my breath with that damn smile. "Of course. Anything you want. I'm your man." His smirk gets bigger and I almost die, but somehow, I get through my next statement.

"If I go with you, you'll need to be my date for my parents' anniversary."

"I'm a big hit with parents."

I find that statement dubious. The man looks like walking sin, built for pleasure. There's no way any father would like his daughter dating this sex-on-legs beefcake. The moms... They're a different story. I could see him being a total winner with anyone with a vagina between her legs. This man could probably make the deadest womb come alive, begging to be impregnated.

"When's your party?"

"This Saturday."

"I think I'm free," I lie.

I don't want to admit the sad truth of my life—that I'm free every night. The only thing I had planned this weekend was to finish bingeing my newest guilty pleasure alone on my couch.

"Perfect. It's a date, but not a date, then. Let me give you my number."

"For what?" I ask.

"Um." He laughs softly and shrugs. "In case you have any questions."

"I can just walk over and ask."

"I'm not always home, and I want you to be able to get ahold of me if you need to. Just take my number, please." He's practically begging, which I like.

"Hold on." I turn my back, walking to the couch slowly so I don't seem overeager to have his number. I've tried to seem as uninterested as possible since I met him. I thought I was winning until now.

When I turn back around after grabbing my phone, I catch the hottie checking out my ass. I'd be lying if I said I wasn't flattered. I've done enough squats to be able to bounce a dime off the damn thing without having any jiggle.

He holds out his hand as I approach. "Let me add my number." He wiggles his fingers before I hand it to him. "Cute," he says as he glances down at my screen, which has a picture of a man much like him, all muscles and tattoos and very little clothing.

"Just put your number in." I lift up on my tiptoes to see what he's doing, but he's too damn tall for me to see anything.

After a few quick taps on the screen, the song "Sexy MF" by Prince starts to play from the pocket of his gray sweat pants, and my gaze dips to the sound.

Big mistake.

There's something about gray sweat pants that shows off every inch of a man. Every fucking delicious inch. Between his bare, muscular chest and whatever he's packing in those sweats, my body's reminding me that I am, in fact, very much alive and horny as fuck.

"Now you have my number, and I have yours." He holds my phone out to me, but I'm too taken by his body to move. Namely the extremely visible outline of his above-average cock.

When I bring my gaze back to his, he's very much amused by the fact that I was checking out his well-defined package. "Just let me know when and where." I grimace because that sounded way more sexual than I'd planned, but based on the smirk dancing across his lips, he liked it.

"I'll pick you up. I'll text you the time as soon as I double-check with my boss."

"What should I wear?" I suddenly feel panicked.

"Whatever you want. I'm sure you're a knockout in anything."

My face heats, and the dull ache between my legs becomes a full-on throb.

Do not go there, Bianca. He thinks you're a knockout.

"I'll let you get back to—" he pauses and looks around me at the television screen "—*Scandalous Reign*."

"Wait. You know this show?"

He smirks, and I can't help but stare at his beautiful full lips. "I binged it last month."

I narrow my eyes, and I wonder, who is this man? No one I know watches this show besides chicks—and, typically, only lonely ones like me.

"I get it," I say, all the pieces finally clicking together. "You're gay and need a female date."

He staggers backward like I punched him in the gut. "What? No. Why would you think that?" He's looking at me like I have two heads, but it's the only thing that makes logical sense to me.

A guy like Vinnie could have any woman on his arm. There's probably a line of bimbos waiting outside right now, wanting a ride on the Vinnie pleasure train. Instead, he's at my door, the door of a complete stranger, begging me to go to his company's dinner? So weird.

"Guys don't usually watch this show, and you don't need to ask a stranger on a date."

"My mother and sister got me into that show." He blushes, and it's so completely adorable, I nearly go weak in the knees. "What can I say? I'm a sucker for a good romance."

"So, you're straight?" I blurt out because I need to

hear the words again. Part of me wishes he'd say he's gay because having a neighbor this hot during my self-imposed celibacy period is bad.

His stare intensifies, and I swear to fuck, his cock twitches in his pants, but I don't dare look down, so I only see the movement in my peripheral vision. "I'm as straight as they come. I'm all man, baby."

"I have to go." I need to get away from him.

Away from his big, rippling muscles.

Away from his magical, jumping cock.

And away from the half-naked body I'll be thinking about when I touch myself later.

"I'll text you," he says with a quick chin lift.

I nod but don't speak.

I can't.

There's nothing I can say that won't come out sounding all wanton and horny. My body's buzzing, my pussy is begging for action, and I know I'm fucked—and not in the way Princess Viktoria is about to be on my new favorite television show.

He just stands there, watching me with those piercing green eyes as I close the door.

"Well," I say into the emptiness of my loft, knowing what's about to come out of my mouth is a partial truth. "Thanks, universe. You've fucked me."

CHAPTER 4
VINNIE

"WHAT'S WITH THE FACE?" Angelo sets down a beer in front of Carlos, but his eyes are on me.

I haven't even made it more than two steps inside the bar, and my brother's already calling me out. "It's pretty, isn't it? You're jealous, aren't you?"

He shakes his head before leaning over the bar, chewing on the toothpick which has become a new habit of his. "You look like someone killed your puppy."

Carlos turns on his stool, glancing at me. "You look like shit, kid." He's never one to hold back his opinions. "Girl problems?"

I groan as I straddle the stool next to Carlos and somehow avoid smashing my head into the wood below my hands. "It's Tracie."

"That bitch is wackadoo." Carlos shakes his head. "Sometimes nutty can be good in the sack. You know?"

I do know. There isn't a person on the planet

who hasn't had a half-insane person rocking the sheets of their bed at one time or another. For a moment, it's easy to think you can deal with the lunatic because the fucking is so good, but once the orgasm strikes and the nut comes out, it's time to ditch the shell and choose being alone over the roller coaster ride.

Angelo pulls the toothpick from between his teeth and glares at Carlos for a second. "You're really fucked up sometimes." Then he turns to me, and his face softens. "She still pulling shit?"

"She never stopped. I have one final Hail Mary." Carlos snorts at the football reference, but I keep talking and ignore him. "I have a date for the team party. Coach said I need to be seen in public with someone because Tracie's been spouting off at the mouth about how we're a couple."

"Pushing crazy's buttons is never a good thing," Carlo warns before taking a sip of his beer. "You're poking the bear, kid. Gonna get bit."

"Is that smart?" Angelo asks, ignoring Carlos too because we both know he's almost as nuts as Tracie.

I rest my elbow against the bar and drag my hand down my face. "Coach said I needed to do it, so I did it."

Angelo points at me. "Try not to take one of your bimbos."

"Give me some credit, will ya?"

He lifts an eyebrow, knowing me better than I probably know myself.

"I found someone respectable to take with me. Someone I haven't even slept with yet."

"Oh, this is about to get good." Carlos smacks his lips together. "Real good."

"You have anything to add besides commentary?" I give Carlos the side-eye.

He shakes his head, going back to his beer but mumbling something I can't quite make out against the glass.

Angelo reaches under the counter and grabs a glass, holding it out to me, but I shake my head. "Who's the woman?" he asks.

"My neighbor."

"What's she do?"

"Fuck if I know." I shrug.

I haven't even bothered to ask, nor do I care because it doesn't matter. I needed a rescue, and her name was the first thing that slipped through my lips.

I can feel the weight of Angelo's eyes as he fills his glass with soda. "I don't know, kid. I hope Carlos is wrong about this, but you could be opening a whole new can of worms."

"The coach has assured me Tracie'll be dealt with."

Angelo's about to take a sip, but he pauses with the glass just in front of his mouth. "She's the owner's granddaughter, dumbass. How's he going to deal with her? Family's family."

"Yeah, but money's money, and Mr. Turner is all about bringing a championship to the city."

Angelo nods, knowing what I'm saying is partially

right. But then, he's right too. Family is family. There're only so many ways you can deal with a problem caused by someone you love.

"Well, I hope it works," he says.

"What's wrong?" Ma says, finally showing her face after she's been hiding on the stairwell, eavesdropping.

"We know you've been listening. What's your advice?"

She sits down on the stool next to me and grabs my face. "Want me to talk to Mr. Turner?"

Angelo nearly doubles over in laughter.

"What? No, Ma," I say quickly.

Betty Gallo has no boundaries. She'd do anything for the people she loves, even if it means embarrassing the hell out of them.

"You'll always be my baby. I can be very convincing." She smiles, running her thumb down the side of my cheek.

"That'll go over big in the locker room." Angelo tries to catch his breath, but he only laughs harder.

I pull her hands away from my face and place them in her lap. "Ma, I got this covered. Really, I do. Let me handle this."

"I should've taken care of that girl after Vegas. Disgraceful," Ma mutters, shaking her head. "You said you had it handled then, but it seems you didn't."

The entire family got their first full taste of Tracie when she showed up at the palatial suite I rented for the draft. Not only did she drop by without being asked, but when my ma answered the door, Tracie had on a trench coat, which was open, and nothing else underneath.

Pop was amused, but Ma had nothing but harsh words, waving her arms in the air as she chased the trust-fund baby down the hallway all the way to the elevator.

"I did, Ma. I'm handling it, but I had to prove myself first. Please, for the love of God, do not do anything."

"Baby, I'm always going to do right by you." Ma gives me a sweet, innocent smile.

Doing right and minding her own business are two entirely different things. My mother tends to be cagey with her answers when she's already cooking up a plan in her mind.

I stare at my mother, totally not amused. "That's not a no, Ma. Promise me you won't do anything."

"Fine." She sighs. "How do you plan on getting rid of her?"

"Coach's got it covered," I tell her. She raises an eyebrow, and I know she wants more. "There's a team party Friday night. I have to bring a date with me to show that Tracie and I are not an item. Then, he'll talk to Mr. Turner about Tracie and figure out a solution to make everyone happy."

Ma doesn't speak as she moves her head from side to side like she's having an internal debate. "I don't know," she mumbles under her breath. "It could work, but doubtful. Who's your date?"

"It's..."

She places her hand over my mouth, stopping me

from saying Bianca's name. "I have the perfect date for you. Emma Claire."

I gag behind her palm as soon as I hear the name. Emma Claire is a nice girl, but nothing about her is attractive to me. "There's no way I'm taking Emma Claire."

My mother smacks my cheek playfully. "She's a nice girl. Hush your mouth."

"Isn't she studying to be a nun?" Angelo asks, knowing our ma is being ridiculous for even bringing up her name.

Ma glares at Angelo. "What's wrong with that? She's a good girl."

Angelo holds up his hands. "Ma, I don't think professional football players are a good fit for Emma Claire and her prayers. That's all. She's too good of a girl for one of those parties."

"Scrap Emma Claire. It's not happening, Ma. No one who knows me will believe I'm dating Emma Claire."

"Fine. Who's the girl you're taking, then? Which bimbo is it this time?"

"My neighbor Bianca."

"Ahh," she sings. "A good Italian girl."

"Nope. A spicy Latina."

"Catholic?" she fires back.

"I don't know." I look at her funny because what the hell does it matter what religion she is. "We're not getting married. We're swapping dates."

"Swapping dates?" She gawks at me and then at Angelo like he has the answer, but he only shrugs.

"She's coming with me to the party, and I'm going with her to her parents' anniversary dinner."

"Is that what your generation has come to?" she asks with a sour look on her face.

"I don't even know what that means. We're helping each other out."

"What's her last name?"

Jesus. I feel like I'm being grilled by a Chicago detective. "I don't know."

She glances up toward the ceiling and mutters some Gaelic curse word. "Maybe I should meet this girl."

Angelo waves his hand to me. "Ma, let the man handle it. He's a big boy now."

She grabs my shoulders and stares me straight in the eyes. "This girl could be some unbalanced stalker."

"Tracie is the stalker, Ma. Bianca is a neighbor who's made it very clear she's not into me."

"She's playing hard to get."

"Betty," Tilly says as she opens the front door of the bar, rescuing me. "Can you help me for a minute?"

"We're not done," Ma tells me before she slides off the barstool and heads toward Tilly.

"You can thank me later for the save." Angelo taps the wooden bar top in front of me.

"She's brutal." I shake my head, wishing our mother didn't always feel the need to butt into our lives.

"She means well, but she gets carried away."

I nod at my brother. "I better run. I have some shit to do before my shift tonight. I'll be back on time."

He lifts an eyebrow, and I know he doesn't believe

me. "You're always late. You'll be late to your own funeral."

"I'll be here at seven."

"Six, dumbass. Don't play games. Tate has ballet class tonight."

For my niece, I'll be on time. That girl has me wrapped around her little finger. I don't know how my brother says no to her because I sure as fuck can't. Never have been and never will be able to either.

I walk around the back of the building to get to my car, avoiding passing by the large windows in front of the cupcake shop. I'll go to any length not to have my mother coming after me again, serving up Emma Claire to me once more.

I make my way to Macy's for a new shirt since all of mine are in boxes somewhere and probably won't see the light of day until God knows when. Between training camp and then the football season, not much is going to get accomplished.

Other than football, my life is a mess. I thought playing college ball was bad, but it's nothing compared to the workouts and training at the professional level.

CHAPTER 5
BIANCA

I'VE SPENT most of the week staring at a blank computer screen. The words I need so badly aren't coming, and no matter how hard I try, I can't seem to think about anything except my very hot and often partially clothed neighbor.

I've tried every yoga pose in the book and running on the treadmill until my body is exhausted, but nothing gets my mind off the muscle-clad green-eyed man who's just a few feet away.

He's been quiet since he moved in. Something I told him I wanted and needed, but it didn't help keep me focused. Even hours upon hours of *Scandalous Reign* have been useless in helping my naughty creativity.

"How's your manuscript coming?" Susan, my agent, asks after she calls me out of the clear blue.

"Fantastic," I lie because I don't want her to go berserk. I'm putting enough pressure on myself; I don't need to add her panic on top of mine.

"The deadline to the publisher is in five weeks," she reminds me, as if I could've forgotten.

"I know. I know."

"Foreign publishers are already interested. This could be the biggest one yet, Bianca."

No pressure there or anything.

"That's great." There's no enthusiasm in my voice.

"What's wrong?"

"Nothing, Susan. Everything's just great."

"Why don't you send me what you've written so far, and I'll read over it and send you some notes."

I stare at the three dresses I have draped across my bed, debating how sexy would be appropriate for tonight's party. "I'd rather wait until I'm finished. I don't want anything messing with my mojo."

"I understand," she says, but she has no idea there's actually nothing to send her. "I'd like to see some of the new chapters by next week."

"I have to go. I'm running late."

I've always hit my deadlines, but rarely am I early. I thought swearing off men would help me write, but I was completely wrong, and I'm paying for it now.

"Where are you going?" I can hear the surprise in her voice. She knows my schedule better than I do, especially since my life has become predictably boring.

"A party with a friend."

"A male friend?" she asks because she's always been nosy as fuck.

I pick up the red dress and hold it against my body

as I stare into the full-length mirror next to my closet. "He needed a plus one for a work party."

"Work parties are the worst," she groans.

"Thanks for keeping the excitement alive, Susan. You always know how to lift my spirits."

She laughs. "Maybe you'll find some inspiration."

"Uh, yeah."

She doesn't realize how much inspiration I need to find to finish this damn book. Vinnie hasn't been inspirational so far. I do find myself daydreaming about his naked chest and those damn gray sweat pants, but they never lead to words on the page.

"Okay. Go get ready. Keep me posted on your progress. I'll call again in a week if I don't hear from you."

"I'd expect nothing less."

I could go months without hearing from Susan, but the closer I get to a deadline, the more and more she texts, emails, and calls.

"Bye, Bianca."

"Later, Susan," I say quickly before tossing my phone onto the bed, needing to get ready.

The red dress is the only thing in my closet that's classy and sexy but not trashy. The rest of my wardrobe is filled with comfy clothes or workout gear, none of which would be appropriate tonight. I pull the dress up over my hips and reach my hand behind my back, unable to find the zipper. I groan, hating these moments where I don't have an extra set of hands to zip me up.

My hair is spot-on in an updo with some crystal-studded bobby pins to add a little sparkle to my brown locks. I'm wearing more makeup than I have since my cousin Vivian was married last year. The smoky eye took me two tries and watching a YouTube video to nail completely.

I step back, staring at myself in the mirror and wondering if it's the right look for the party. I never asked what he did, and maybe I've gone a little too sexy if he's something boring like an accountant or a teacher.

When there's a knock on the door, my heart rate doubles and nerves set in. There's no time to second-guess or change. "You've got this," I tell myself as I smooth down the front of my dress. "You look good."

Matt, my last boyfriend, was hell on my ego. The man spent more time nitpicking things he felt were my flaws than complimenting me. Any extra ounce of fat on my body and he'd take every opportunity to grab on to it, reminding me I needed to work out more. He was obsessed with looks, and mine never seemed to be good enough for him.

He's the reason I swore off men, deciding to focus more on my work than his unrealistic expectations of beauty.

"Coming!" I yell when there's a second knock. I take a deep breath and remind myself this is only a favor, nothing more.

It's easier not to have any expectations. If I don't expect anything from tonight, there's no way I can be let down.

As soon as I open the door, my tongue nearly lodges

itself in my throat. My neighbor looked hot as fuck half naked when he stood at my door the other day. But damn it, the way the man wears a dress shirt and pants is nothing short of spectacular.

"Wow," he says as his eyes sweep down my body. "You look amazing."

My belly flips at the compliment. "You clean up nice," I tell him, trying to play it cool when my body is damn near close to overheating.

The way he has the sleeves rolled up his forearms makes my toes curl. I'm a sucker for muscles, and this guy has them everywhere.

"Can you zip me up?" I ask, turning around because I need a moment to freak out without him seeing my face.

I can feel his body heat as he steps closer. When his hand touches the zipper and his other hand rests on my hip, my knees nearly give out. I'm way too horny, and I realize going without dick for six months probably wasn't my smartest idea. Never have I been so turned on by such a simple touch.

His fingers dig into the skin on my hip, and I can feel the power in his grip. "Cute tattoo," he says with his mouth so close to my ear, I shiver.

"I lost a bet." I manage to get the words out, but barely. "I had to get it. I figured at least I couldn't see it on my lower back."

"But I can," he says, his voice deep and husky. "It's hot." His fingertips graze my spine as he pulls the zipper upward at an agonizingly slow pace.

"What about your ink?" I'd admired it the other day as he stood half naked in my doorway, and I wasn't about to ask then.

"The eagle, flag, and ND are for my country and my alma mater. The dream catcher to remind me of my goals and making them a reality. There's no real hidden meaning in them."

"They look good on you."

The zipper's all the way up, but his hand still lingers on my waist. I concentrate on my breathing and not the dull ache that's already starting between my legs because this hot-as-fuck guy is standing so near with his hands on me.

"Bianca," he whispers as he moves a little closer.

I hold my breath and stay silent.

He takes a step forward, almost pressing his body against mine. "I haven't been completely honest with you."

I try to turn around, but he tightens his grip on my waist and stops me. "About?" My skin breaks out in goose bumps.

"Don't get mad, but..." he starts, and my belly flutters again, "I may have told everyone you're my girlfriend. To make it believable, I'm probably going to have to touch you tonight. I don't want you to deck me if I try to hold your hand or put my arm around your waist."

"Oh."

My mind's spinning, wondering why a guy as good-looking as he is has to lie about having a girlfriend. I'm pretty sure women throw themselves at him, offering up their bodies for his pleasure. I've never been one to go all gaga over a guy, but with the way he's touching me, I'm pretty close to ditching the party and asking him to fuck me so I can get over my sexless slump.

"Is it going to be okay if I touch you?" he asks.

I pause, pretending I'm thinking about it, but I want to scream out *Yes, touch me, please.* Instead, I nod and take a deep breath before speaking. "Yes. I'll tell you if it's too much."

But at this point, I'm not sure there is such a thing as too much. I wonder if I'd been with someone in the last six months, would Vinnie affect me in the same way he is right now? Who am I kidding? This guy is off-the-charts hot, and with all the rippling muscles, he's made for pleasure.

"I promise to be a gentleman and to respect you, but I can't keep my hands to myself tonight. My job is on the line here."

"Okay," I whisper. A little part of me is sad. I want him to touch me because he wants to, not because he has to. At least he's up front about it, so I don't get my hopes up or get the wrong idea.

"Every guy in the place is going to be jealous of me, too. No one's girl is as beautiful as you."

My face heats as his words wash over me. "You don't have to butter me up, Vinnie. A deal is a deal."

Both of his hands are now at my waist as he spins me around to face him. "I'm not buttering you up," he says, piercing my soul with those emerald eyes. "I'm being serious. You're a total knockout."

"I don't look chunky in this?"

Chunky is a word Matt used often. I am curvy with lush hips, an hourglass figure, and an ass Jennifer Lopez would be proud of.

Vinnie looks confused. "Chunky?"

"Yeah. Like, fat. Do I look fat in this?"

"You look edible in that dress." His fingers tighten on my waist, and all the air in the room seems to disappear. "If this event weren't so important and you actually liked me, I'd already be worshiping your body."

"Pretty sure of yourself, aren't you?" I tease, trying to pretend like my body isn't wishing he'd rip off my dress and bury his face between my legs.

"Baby..." he says again.

I've always hated that cute little pet name, but somehow it doesn't sound so bad coming out of his mouth when he's talking to me.

"I can be very convincing." He winks.

I swallow, but my mouth is suddenly drier than any desert I've ever been to. All I can do is stare at him, blinking and wondering how he is in bed. *Don't go there. He's just like the others.*

"Your car or mine?" I ask, trying to change the subject before I do or say something that ends with us in my bed, breaking the promise I made to myself.

"We'll take mine."

"I have a pretty fun car," I tell him.

I have a ridiculous payment and barely ever drive

the thing. It was a luxury item and something I couldn't resist purchasing after always dreaming of owning something so frivolous.

"For your party, you can drive. But tonight, let me be the man."

Ah. The macho attitude. Some guys have got it, while others are completely lacking the gene. "So, it's your job to drive?"

He shakes his head. "It's my job to take care of you. Let me spoil you, even if it's only for an evening."

The man says all the right things. I'm independent, probably too much sometimes. But there are moments when I want to let go and let someone else handle things. Tonight, I'm going to let Vinnie be the man, and I'm going to enjoy every worry-free moment.

"Just for tonight," I agree.

When his hands leave my body, I instantly miss his touch and the sweet bite of his warm, strong fingertips against my skin.

Maybe this wasn't the best idea, but it's too late to turn back now.

CHAPTER 6
VINNIE

"IS THERE a beefy-guy breeding farm I don't know about somewhere around here?" Bianca asks as soon as we walk into the ballroom at the Ritz.

I laugh, glancing around the room with her and realizing almost everyone is as built as me. Some have a little more padding, but no one is small except the coaching staff.

"We have to be big."

She looks over her shoulder at me. "What exactly do you do?"

I smile, feeling proud to be able to say for the first time that I've achieved the one goal I've been working my ass off for years. "I play football."

"Like football, football?"

"What other football is there?"

"Gallo," my coach says as soon as he sees us. "This must be the beautiful Bianca I've heard so much about."

I give Bianca a smile. "This is," I say with a hand on

the small of her back, loving the way she feels in my arms.

"It's lovely to meet you. Vinnie speaks very highly of you," Coach Malik tells her without looking at me as he holds out his hand for Bianca.

She places her palm in his hand, before he leans over and kisses the skin on the back of her hand. My body tightens at the contact, and my hand slides around to her side, pulling her closer.

"Coach," I grumble, knowing he's only being a gentleman, but not liking it just the same.

"I'll let you two get settled. Grab a drink and mingle." He smiles, still staring at Bianca.

Looking around the room, I know she's the best-looking woman here. She's naturally beautiful. Stunning, even. The other team wives have had so much Botox, their faces barely move anymore. Between the injections and the plastic surgeries, I'm pretty sure they look nothing like the women their husbands fell in love with years ago.

"Wait," Bianca says as soon as the coach walks away from us. "Who are you?"

"Vinnie Gallo. Hopefully the newest starting quarterback for Chicago."

She goes to back up, but I hold her tightly. "You're a professional football player," she whispers.

"I'm a rookie. I was just drafted."

She blinks. "Shit. I watched that draft with my brothers and my dad. I remember you."

"I'm kind of unforgettable." I smirk.

"I did forget," she teases with a small smile. "But now I remember. My family was psyched, screaming at the television like idiots when your name was called."

"Did you scream my name too?"

"No." She laughs.

"You will." I tighten my grip on her waist again.

Her face instantly turns red, but she doesn't tell me to fuck off, so I'd say I'm winning. Being with Bianca tonight has been easy so far. Maybe it's the fact that neither of us is expecting anything out of the night, but whatever it is, I like it. She isn't like the other women I've been with. She doesn't want anything from me.

"Who do we have here?" Clarence asks, interrupting the moment.

"This is Bianca," I tell him, and I wave my hand in his direction. "Bianca, this asshole is Clarence."

He smacks my chest, and I flinch. "I'm his best friend on the team. Don't listen to the idiot," Clarence says.

Bianca's eyes grow bigger. "It's such an honor to meet you, sir. I'm a huge fan."

For some reason, I'm jealous of Clarence. I want Bianca to be a huge fan of me, not him. I want my name to be the one she's chanting on Sunday, not Harris.

"Vinnie should bring you to practice."

I won't be bringing her to practice. Even bringing her here with all these cheating bastards wasn't the best idea I've ever had. The girl isn't even mine, and I already don't want anyone trying to take her from me.

Maybe the hit I took yesterday in practice was harder than I thought.

"That would be amazing," Bianca says with a smile.

"We'll talk about it." My voice is flat, and my hand still hasn't left her body.

Clarence raises an eyebrow, maybe catching my vibe.

"It's not really a place for ladies."

"Stop being a pussy." He smacks me again. "Bring the pretty lady with you someday."

"The pretty lady may not want to be around a bunch of sweaty assholes." I clench my teeth together, wishing Clarence would shut the fuck up.

Bianca smirks. "This lady would very much love to come to practice." She turns to face Clarence. "I've never minded a little sweat." She winks, and I almost die.

"We'll talk about it," I mumble.

She slides her arm around my waist, holding me like I'm holding her. Her fingernails bite into my side. "Honey, I'd love to see where you work," she says with a fake smile, not moving her teeth when she speaks.

"Baby." I flex my fingers into her soft, lush waist.

"Vinnie." The voice makes me cringe.

Clarence's eyes widen. "Shit's about to get real."

"What is this bimbo doing here?" Tracie asks, staring at Bianca like she's nothing but trash.

"This is my girlfriend," I say proudly.

Tracie's eyes slice to me. "I'm your girl."

Bianca stiffens in my arms. "Maybe I should go,"

she says and tries to break free from my hold.

I shake my head, holding her tighter, not letting her leave. "Don't move," I tell Bianca before glaring at Tracie. "I don't know what part of 'We're nothing' you don't seem to understand, Tracie. We are not a couple. I'm very much taken, as you can see."

Tracie's mouth gapes open. "We'll see about that," she says before she stalks off, tossing her hair over her shoulder like she's about to throw down.

"Who is that?" Bianca asks, jutting her chin toward Tracie as she walks away in a complete tizzy.

Clarence points in Tracie's direction and shakes his head slowly. "That's nothing but crazy."

"So, you have a stalker?" Bianca doesn't seem amused. "Don't you think that's something you should've told me?"

"She's the owner's granddaughter."

Bianca's mouth forms a perfect O. "Well, that's awkward."

"No, that's insanity in heels." Clarence laughs.

"Great," Bianca mumbles, but she doesn't relax. "You threw me right in the path of a nutty chick? Thanks a-fucking-lot."

"Clarence, can you give us a minute?" I ask, feeling like I need to explain all the shit that's gone down over the last six months.

"Sure. We're in the back, and Marquita saved two seats at our table for you."

I give him a chin lift, wishing I didn't have to waste another minute on Tracie. "Thanks, man."

He's barely five feet away when Bianca moves out of my grip and faces me, eyes narrowed and expression totally pissed off.

"I'm your crazy-chick repellent?" She puts her hands on her hips, and I know she wants to clock me. "Are you fucking mad?"

I run my hand through my hair, feeling like an asshole. "The coach said I needed to make a very public statement that Tracie and I were and never will be a couple. He told me to bring my girlfriend with me to prove to Mr. Turner that his granddaughter is indeed off-the-rails insane again."

"Again?" Her mouth hangs open. "She has a history of this shit?"

"She has a history of stalking players."

Her shoulders bunch up near her head like she's a volcano about to blow. "I'm your bait, aren't I? I should knock your ass out right here," she says in a low, scary voice, and I feel like she could do it if given half a chance.

She's so damn hot when she's mad, too.

"You're my saving grace." I reach for her, but she slaps my hand and pulls away.

"Don't."

"Bianca, come on. Don't be that way." I take a step toward her, wanting nothing more than to smooth things over.

She stops moving away from me. "You should've warned me, Vinnie."

"Would you have come?"

"I don't know, but at least I would've had a choice."

"She's gone now. She won't be a problem," I promise her, but I don't know if it's entirely true. "Don't let her ruin our evening. I was enjoying myself until she showed up."

"So was I."

This time, I move faster than her, wrapping my arms around her back and locking my fingers together. Our bodies are touching, and she feels fucking spectacular in my arms.

"Do you like me?" I ask point-blank.

"What?" She doesn't fight me or my hold.

"Do. You. Like. Me?" I ask again.

"I… Uh…"

I flatten my palms against her back. "It's an easy question, Bianca. Are you attracted to me?"

She blushes.

"I'm attracted to you," I say with complete honesty. This may have started as a favor, but there's no one else I'd rather be here with.

She glances up at me, and there's sadness in her eyes for a moment before it passes. "I don't think I'm really your type. You probably want some skinny supermodel."

I stare at her, dumbfounded by her statement. "The last thing I want is some twig at my side. I'm a big boy, and sometimes I can be rough." I can see her swallow as the vein in her neck starts to pulse quicker. "You are very much my type, and I like you, too. Big attitude and all."

"You like me?" She looks surprised.

I don't get why she'd believe any differently. I think I've made myself pretty clear in the limited amount of time we've spent together. Why would a woman as pretty as Bianca think a guy wouldn't want her? It makes no sense.

I nod. "Very much."

"Son," a man says behind me, touching my shoulder.

I turn my head, finding the owner watching us. "Mr. Turner, sir."

"This must be the lovely Bianca." There's a genuine smile on his face as he lays eyes on the girl in the beautiful red dress.

"How many people did you tell about me?" she whispers in my ear, sending tiny shock waves through my system as her warm breath caresses my skin.

"This is indeed my girl Bianca, sir," I say again, but this time, she doesn't stiffen in my arms.

"Well, aren't you a sight for sore eyes. A natural beauty," he tells her with a dip of his head. "I hope you're a Chicago fan."

"I am." Bianca smiles and absolutely lights up the room.

"I hope to see you at some games this year. I'm sure the ladies would like someone new to gossip with." He grabs my shoulder. "And this boy has them all buzzing. He's going to bring us a championship. I can feel it in my bones."

"Sir," I say with a dip of my head, loving the hell out

of him, but needing his help. "I want to talk to you about Tracie."

He shakes his head. "She's being dealt with. You worry about the field, the ball, and your girl. Leave everything else to me."

"Thank you, sir."

"You built up an entire story about me?" Bianca asks as soon as Mr. Turner is far enough away that he can't hear us.

"I didn't have a choice." I shrug.

"Why me? Why my name?" She crosses her arms over her chest.

I tuck my hand into my pocket and try to be cool and calm, hoping I don't sound like the biggest wanker in the world for what I'm about to say. "After we met in the elevator, I couldn't stop thinking about you. When they asked about my girlfriend, your name was the first that came out of my mouth because, again, I was thinking about you nonstop."

"About me?" She touches her chest, looking shocked that I actually would've been thinking about her.

"Yeah, and the thoughts weren't always pure, but damn, they were hot."

The corner of her mouth twitches. "What would you have done if I'd said I wouldn't come with you?"

"I would've been screwed and had to make up some story about how you were home with the flu or that I found you in bed with another man."

She shakes her head and laughs. "That would be an

ego hit, no? No man actually wants to admit they found their woman in bed with another man."

"Finding your woman in bed with another woman is an even bigger ego hit, baby."

She laughs loudly, tipping her head back and exposing her beautiful neck. I want to lean forward and run my lips across the silky-soft skin, but I'm pretty sure Bianca would not hesitate to smack me in front of everyone.

"That would be a complete suck, wouldn't it?" she asks. "Has that happened to you?"

"Nah." I shake my head. "I've never really been with a girl long enough to let it happen."

Her smile vanishes. "What? You've never dated anyone?"

"I go on dates. I just don't do relationships. I don't like the way my heart feels when they end. I've stayed focused on my work and have put off love until later."

"You sound like me." She steps forward, closing the space between us. "I've sworn off men."

"Forever?" I pray like hell she hasn't switched teams.

"For a short time. It was affecting my work."

"And now?" I'm hopeful, and I know maybe a little time with Vinnie will get her head back in the game.

"Now…" She pauses and runs her hands up my arms. "I'm thinking maybe it's time to put myself out there again."

CHAPTER 7
BIANCA

WHAT AM I SAYING? I'm flirting with this guy, a person I barely know and someone I know is a player. Ready to throw away my promise to be celibate, man-free, and drama-free for as long as humanly possible. I've stayed strong for six months, barely leaving my apartment because the temptation only grew stronger over time.

"I could help you," he offers, looking hopeful as he peers down at me, his hands on my hips. "Or maybe we can help each other."

"Help each other?" My grip tightens on his biceps.

I'm completely feeling him up in front of all these people. I'm not even ashamed, and he seems to be enjoying it. I've never felt arms so big, and I imagine he could easily lift me off the ground.

He nods. "I'll help you get back in the game, teaching you which assholes to avoid, and you can teach me how to be in a relationship without being such a self-absorbed dick."

I laugh, but I like the idea. "I'm not sure anyone can be taught how to be in a relationship. Plus, I haven't had much luck, so I don't know if I'm the best teacher."

For five years, I've had nothing but a string of shitty boyfriends. One after another, parading through my life like an endless season of bad reruns just with a different leading man. Kind of like in soap operas where they hire a new actor to play the same role. That's been my love life in a nutshell.

"Well, one thing I know is assholes." He smiles. "I can pick them out in a crowd in a few seconds."

"Does it take one to know one?" I tease.

When I met Vinnie, I would've sworn he was a complete tool. But after the short amount of time I've spent with him, I'd say I was completely off base. I might still be right, though. Like I said...my asshole-finder is completely broken. But so far, he's been nothing but a gentleman and sweet, too.

"I've never been an asshole, but that doesn't mean I've always treated women the way they expected or wanted to be treated."

I raise an eyebrow. "How does that not make you an asshole?"

"I never lie to them. I'm always honest about what I want. It's their choice if they want to be with me, knowing what they know in advance."

"Sounds romantic." I shake my head and laugh again.

He grips me tighter with his fingers. "Maybe you can change me. Show me all the things I've been missing."

"Gallo," his friend, Clarence, yells from a few feet away, ruining the moment. "Get your ass over here."

Vinnie sends his buddy a little nod before giving me his eyes again. "We'll talk about this more later."

I don't know if the butterflies in my stomach are from excitement or my mind's way of saying *take a few steps back and do not get naked with this guy*. My body's all for the skin-on-skin action, having been denied for more months than I thought humanly possible. I can feel my resistance slipping.

The promise I made to myself is becoming less and less important.

I try to take a step backward, but Vinnie pulls me close again, keeping his arm around my back and his hand firmly on my hip. "Just remember, everyone in this room thinks we're a couple."

"Got it." My body tingles with every step, soaking in his warmth and the feel of his hands on my body as we walk.

It's not hard to pretend with him.

There are three couples sitting at the table, and all their eyes are on us as we approach. I can feel the weight of their stares as they appraise me. Maybe it's just in my head. I always assume people who have achieved some sort of celebrity have a bit of snob in them.

"Bianca, this is Marquita, Clarence's wife." Vinnie motions toward a beautiful woman who oozes class.

Marquita dips her head. "So, you're the one who's trying to tame our young Vinnie." She laughs and covers her mouth with her hand, showing off the giant diamond ring on her finger.

"He's a tough one, but he's mine." I pat his chest, wishing I could slink away and out of the room. My smile isn't genuine, but somehow, I keep it on my face until my cheeks hurt.

"Don't listen to her," a blond woman says as she waves her hand toward Marquita. "We're excited to finally meet you. I'm Celia, Tre's wife."

Tre is the hottest player on the team. My brothers have his jersey and wear it religiously every Sunday during the season because they think it'll bring the team luck. It doesn't, but that doesn't stop them.

"It's lovely to meet you," I say to Celia.

Celia is beautiful but without all the surgical intervention like Marquita has. Her smile seems genuine and warm, which puts me a little bit at ease.

"Sit. Sit," another woman says and pulls out the chair next to her. "We've all known each other for years and are excited to have someone new at our table for a change."

"Thank you." I slide onto the chair as ladylike as I can in a dress this tight. My usual drop and plop probably wouldn't be a big hit with this crowd.

"I'm Marilou, and this big lug is my husband." She bumps the man next to her, and I immediately know who he is from the years of sitting with my dad and brothers on Sunday afternoon.

"I'm Maurice," he says, giving me a killer smile.

My belly's flipping because I've watched these men for years, and they're celebrities in my family.

"It's wonderful to meet you all," I say.

And it is, except for Marquita. Her face is so pinched, she looks like she just ate something sour. Maybe she just doesn't like me or the fact that Vinnie and I are getting all the attention from the table and not her.

Vinnie sits next to me, moving his chair so our hips are touching. I'm momentarily breathless when his hand slides across my thigh before resting there.

"Champagne?" Marquita asks without moving her face because she's had so much plastic surgery. I'm pretty sure it *can't* move, no matter how hard she tries.

"Please." I nod.

"So, what do you do, Bianca?" Celia asks as she rests her chin in her palm. "Are you a kept woman now that Vinnie's signed his first contract?"

Clarence laughs. "Celia, I told you the boy doesn't play for the money. He was already rolling in dough."

I glance over at Vinnie, trying to hide my shock but failing. I figured he had some money. No one can buy a unit above the eighth floor in our building without a substantial bank account.

"It's rude to talk money, especially other people's money," Marquita tells Celia as she pushes the champagne bottle across the table.

Celia rolls her eyes, and I can tell they aren't the best of friends. I'm pretty sure no one at this table counts Marquita on their BFF list.

Vinnie's unusually quiet, and I turn to him, wondering what's running through his mind. He shrugs, giving me a halfhearted smile. "Tell them what you do, baby."

He doesn't even know what I do. We've spent so little time talking about our lives, the topic never even came up. Hell, I didn't even know what he did until we arrived at the event tonight.

I grab the champagne bottle, keeping my eyes trained on the bubbly, filling my glass so I don't have to see their faces. "I'm a writer."

"Like a journalist?" Clarence asks.

Journalist is always everyone's first thought when I say I'm a writer. I'll never understand it. I think so many people believe no one can really make a living by writing novels, especially romance novels, but I do it.

I'm one of the lucky few.

I'm successful.

I shake my head and grab Vinnie's glass and fill it too. "I write novels." I glance upward, seeing the surprise on Vinnie's face.

"I love a good thriller. Maybe I've read your work. What's your last name?" Marquita asks, but I'm pretty sure she's just asking so she can belittle me again.

"I don't think you've read my work."

There's always this awkward moment. They're so interested and full of questions, but as soon as they hear what I write, they'll have nothing but judgment and disdain.

Vinnie's hand tightens on my thigh. He's so damn close to the promised land, I could explode if his hand moved up any higher.

Maurice lifts his glass, watching me over the rim. "You're talking to a bunch of jocks and housewives, sweetheart. We barely write, let alone read."

Marilou wraps her hand around her husband's upper arm. "Honey, you know I read all the time. I have to do something to keep myself busy during the season."

"I love when you read, Mar. I reap the rewards from all those words." She gets a wink from Maurice.

I fidget with the stem of the champagne flute, remaining silent as I watch Maurice and Marilou. They're cute together and so totally in love.

"Please tell me you don't write murder mysteries." Marilou rolls her eyes. "They're so boring and predictable."

"I write romance novels," I blurt out because there's nothing like ripping the Band-Aid off quickly to break the ice and get over the weird moment where everyone looks at me like I'm an easy lay.

That's the thing about being a romance writer. Everyone always assumes I'm some sort of weird nymphomaniac, when I'm the exact opposite. No one makes that assumption about a person who writes crime novels. They don't think they're a career criminal based on the words they put on paper. It's exactly the opposite for romance. We're all slutty harlots, writing from our vast experience of opening our legs for every Tom, Dick, and Harry.

Vinnie's fingers dig into my skin as he gives me a proud smile. "That's my girl."

"Oh my God. I love romance. I devour them. What's your name? I must read your books," Marilou says as the other women gawk at me like I'm some kind of whore, as expected.

"Bianca May." I smile, knowing I should be proud of everything I've accomplished at my age.

I am.

I'm prouder than anyone will ever know, but it's the way people's opinions of me form as soon as they hear "romance" that still punches me square in the gut sometimes.

"Shut your mouth." She gasps. "I've read all of your books. You're one of my favorites."

I can't stop the smile from spreading across my face. "Really?"

It's still shocking when anyone says they love my words. Every novel I finish, there's always doubt in the back of my mind that it's good enough or that my readers will enjoy it.

She nods excitedly. "*Tempted by Fate* is my all-time favorite."

"We have a famous author at our table." Maurice holds out his champagne glass and tips it in my direction. "Do you get your inspiration from Vinnie?"

"I get inspiration from everything and everyone around me."

"Is writing lucrative?" Marquita asks because, of course, the stuck-up bitch is obsessed with money. "I've heard so many stories about how writers can barely afford to pay their bills."

"It can be," I tell her and bite my tongue because I want to tell her to fuck off.

"What do you do to support yourself financially while you write?" she asks with a small smirk because, again...she's a bitch.

I don't usually like to talk about my success and money, especially in front of strangers, but she's such an asshole, I can't think of anything other than putting her in her place. On top of that, I'm sitting at a table filled with professional football players who are paid in the millions. They won't faint at the figures I'm about to throw around.

"My last book made a little over a million dollars." I stare straight at Marquita, hoping she chokes on the champagne she's raising to her lips. "In the first month," I add to drive that little uptight-bitch dagger right into Marquita's heart.

Vinnie rocks back in his chair like he's stunned, and right on cue, Marquita chokes on that damn fancy champagne.

"Wow," Clarence says. "Who knew there was so much money in romance."

I nod, feeling the knots in my stomach finally start to loosen. "It's the hottest-selling genre on the market, with a ravenous and dedicated readership. I have a wonderful publisher, which helps."

Marquita dabs the corner of her mouth with a napkin, careful not to smear her perfect makeup. "Huh," she mumbles into the cloth.

Clarence covers her hand, silencing her before she says another assholish thing. "You must be popular to bring in seven figures with your work."

"She's the best," Marilou tells him. "She's done book tours around the world, and people line up outside the store when her new book releases. She's a rock star."

My face heats at her compliment. "I do okay, but I do it because I love it, not for the money." I've always tried to remain humble, preferring to be alone with my computer and words instead of having readers fawn over me.

Marilou waves her hand at me. "She's being modest."

Vinnie leans over, bringing his mouth right next to my ear. "I'm going to have to read your books now. I want to crawl inside your dirty mind a little bit."

I want to correct him. Tell him that my books are fantasy and nothing more. They're fiction, after all, filled with happy endings and a lot of sex. They're nothing like my real life.

"I think she's a keeper, Gallo," Clarence tells him. "Hold on to this one as tight as possible. It's not often you find a driven, successful woman who's willing to put up with our bullshit."

"I plan to, Clarence. I plan to," Vinnie says in a low, husky voice, sending goose bumps across my skin.

I'm so screwed.

How am I going to meet my deadline with the hot baller next to me trying to creep into my bed?

"Listen to Clarence," ... Vivienne put a hand...
Ruby wine sloshing... in her glass...

... and I'm going to meet... beside with...
better call for back-up to keep... in our side.

CHAPTER 8
VINNIE

I READ over the last paragraph again, visualizing Bianca as the woman in her book.

"Down on your knees," he says, holding her chin tightly between his fingers and staring at her with so much burning desire, her body catches fire.

She kneels gracefully, keeping her eyes fixed on his, loving the way he looks at her like she's the most precious thing in the world.

"Be a good girl and unzip me." He taps her cheek softly.

His words wash over her, bathing her in warmth as her need to feel the velvety hardness of his cock between her lips grows. His zipper comes down easily, and she looks to him for the next command.

"Take my cock out, sweetheart, and show me how much you love me."

Her fingers look so tiny wrapped around his stiff cock. She uses one hand to yank the jeans down his thighs, freeing his hardness from its constraints.

"Take me deep," he tells her, watching her carefully as she palms his length.

She nods, unable to say anything, and not allowed to either. When she steps into the room, she's his to do with what he wants, without reservation.

She's his pet. His property. His fucktoy. She likes being owned, used, and powerless.

"Holy fuck," I whisper, stroking my cock without even realizing I'm doing it. The book is way hotter than I imagined and makes me just as hard as watching any porno. Knowing Bianca wrote the words only makes it all sexier.

The thought of Bianca on her knees as my sex slave does wicked things to my insides and has my cock begging for attention. The words inside this book are dirty as fuck, and I wonder how much is from Bianca's real life or her fantasies.

I tap the screen, flipping the page quickly, needing to know what happens next.

"Do you like that?" he says as she moans around the head of his cock, sending a new sensation skittering across his insides.

His fingers tangle in her hair, forcing her to take more of him, deep-throating his length. She gags, tears spilling from her eyes, but loving every minute of their sexual game.

She rests her hands on her knees as he thrusts his hips forward, taking complete control. Her mouth is just a plea-sure vessel and his for the taking.

His grip tightens, almost painfully, as his spine tingles and the orgasm he's been wanting and needing builds.

By the time he's exploding in her mouth, I'm rock hard and rubbing my cock faster than before.

I squeeze my eyes shut, picturing Bianca's lips wrapped around my dick, sucking me off and taking me deep.

"Fuck," I groan as colors explode behind my eyelids and my body stiffens, the orgasm crashing over me in waves.

Where the hell did that come from?

I can't remember the last time I came so hard or so quickly. Reaching into the depths of Bianca's mind, reading the words she typed with her very own fingers has my head spinning and my body on fire like never before.

After I clean myself up and my breathing goes back to normal, I pick up my phone and think carefully about my next words. I don't want to sound like some asshole who's only after her for some ass, but damn, the girl makes my mind reel with possibilities.

Me: So, I've been reading one of your books. You're an amazing writer.

I roll my eyes as soon as I hit send, knowing I sound like a moron. What else am I supposed to say? I guess I could've stayed quiet, pretended I never read the words in her last novel, but part of me wants her to know.

Bianca: Um…Thanks. Which one?

Me: His. It is hot AF too.

Bianca: Readers seemed to love it.

What's not to love? The guy was powerful yet nice, and the girl was like a Pandora's box of pleasure. I'm only halfway through their story, but I can't imagine the action ever wanes.

Me: *How do you come up with your story ideas?*

Bianca: *Not my real life. That's for sure.*

Me: *Come on. A beautiful girl like you has to have men lining up at the door to take you out.*

Bianca: *Check the hallway. It's empty.*

With that, I'm on my feet, heading toward the hallway because if no one else is going to wait at her door, I sure as fuck will.

Me: *I see a line.*

Bianca: *Ha-ha.*

Me: *No, look.*

Bianca: *No way. I'm not dressed, and I'm working.*

Me: *Even better. ;)*

Bianca: *I'm not home.*

I press my ear against the door, hearing the patter of her feet against the hardwood. I knock lightly and laugh as I hear her running to God knows where.

"Bianca." I lean against the doorframe, talking to the wood that's separating us. "I can hear you in there."

There's nothing but silence. I imagine her stark naked in the middle of her living room, staring at the door.

"I promise I won't bite." I smirk, but fuck do I want to sink my teeth into her soft skin and listen to her moan my name. "I don't care what you're wearing."

Preferably something lacy and sexy. She has to get herself in the mood to write such spectacular sex scenes. She probably sits at her desk, wearing all sorts of lingerie and bright-red painted lips as she pecks away at the keyboard.

The latch to the door lock clicks, and I shove my phone into my pocket, ready to get a look at the sexy romance writer in action.

She opens the door an inch, not giving me much to look at.

"Hey." I smile, keeping my eyes on her face.

"What's up?" Her eyes rake over my bare chest before returning to my face. "I was in the middle of writing a chapter."

"Let me read it," I beg.

"No way."

"Come on." I push against the door a little, but it doesn't budge.

I'm not giving up. I haven't stopped thinking about Bianca since the party the other night. I keep looking for her in the lobby, listening for any movement in the hallway, but she's remained elusive.

"Nope."

"I'm not going anywhere." I fold my arms in front of my chest.

I've never had to work this hard to get a girl to let me into her place. Usually, they're pulling me in the door by my T-shirt, yanking my pants down before we're even in private. But not Bianca. She's the exact opposite, and it's making me curious and crazy.

She rolls her eyes. "You're impossible."

"But I'm adorable too."

She grunts, opening the door and motioning for me

to come in. I stalk into her place, not looking at her until the door shuts. I ready myself for the sexy outfit, the porn star makeup, but I'm met with something entirely different.

She's staring at me with her arms folded, her hair in some weird messy-bun disaster, torn sweat pants, and a coffee-stained T-shirt with the words *Running on Coffee and Dry Shampoo*.

From the looks of her, the shirt's pretty spot-on. It doesn't matter. She's still beautiful. She's still Bianca, the spicy Latina girl with all the dirty thoughts in that pretty mind of hers.

"Happy?" she asks with her face pinched.

"Very much."

"Didn't expect this—" she waves her hands up and down the length of her body "—did you?"

I sweep the hair away from her face. "I don't care what you're wearing, I just wanted to see you."

"You've seen me." She motions toward the door. "You can go now."

"Mama, why so cold?" I run my finger down her cheek, and her pupils dilate as her breathing slows. "I thought you'd be happy to see me. I want to talk about your books."

She steps backward and away from my touch like I'm burning her with the contact. "I'm behind on my deadline, Vinnie, and I'm stuck in this damn scene. I really have to concentrate to nail this part."

My cock twitches, loving the idea of her writing a dirty chapter just as I knocked. Does she get as turned on by her words as the people do who are reading them? I can't imagine having sex on the brain all the time and not touching myself to the point of blacking out.

"Well, I know sex and football. Maybe I can help you work through the scene."

Her tongue darts out, sweeping across her lips as her eyes drift across my chest. "How can you help?"

Instead of going into all the ways I can help her with sex, even in her books, I let her do the talking because I'm about ten seconds from sweeping her off her feet and planting my lips on hers.

"What's the problem?" I ask, praying to God it's something hot.

She starts to pace. "I'm trying to work out the logistics of the position. Keeping all the hands and body parts in the right place is challenging sometimes."

"I'll be your prop. I can help you work out what's happening and where all the body parts should be. Use me."

Her eyes narrow as she looks at me, but she doesn't stop moving back and forth across the room. "I don't know. I've never needed help before, and it might be awkward."

"I'm all about awkward. Remember, I'm a professional too. Let's get you over this hump."

Since I've walked in, we've thrown around words like hump, nail, and other sexual terms that have my body buzzing with excitement.

"Are you sure? You already look a little..." She points to my pants, and my eyes follow.

"Fuck. I'm sorry," I say, pushing my cock downward because, damn it, I'm horny as fuck.

How? I don't know.

Fifteen minutes ago, the orgasm that rocked my body was so hard-core, I wasn't sure I could even get another boner no matter how hard I tried.

Clearly, I was wrong.

Bianca does this to me, and that's how I know I'm in trouble. I should walk away, leave her be, and go back to my place, resting up for practice tomorrow. But I can't. I won't.

"We're not sleeping together," she tells me like she's reading my mind.

"I never thought we were," I lie. "Where do you want me? The bed? The couch?"

She stops moving and stares at me, tapping her chin and not speaking. She chews on the corner of her lip, and I can't stop myself from watching the way the soft skin stretches between her teeth.

"Fine. Come here." She motions for me to follow, and I practically skip across the room out of excitement.

She lies down on the couch with her legs spread and wiggles her fingers as I tower over her. "Get on top of me, but don't get any ideas."

That's laughable. Ask any guy to lie on top of a chick, and his mind is going to be filled with ideas.

"I thought you'd never ask," I say playfully, but fuck me, I really want this girl.

I climb on top of her, careful not to press my hard cock into her pussy. I'm almost certain that would earn me either a slap to the face or a quick escort out of her place.

"Like this?" I balance my weight on one arm, holding my body over her.

She stares up at me with those honey-brown eyes. "Slide your arm under my back and grip my ass, tilting my hips."

I'm in sheer fucking heaven.

"Like this?" My palm finds her soft ass cheek, and I nearly groan at the way she fits perfectly in my hand.

"Exactly like that," she says. "Okay. Now, can you grab the back of my neck with your other hand and still hold up your body weight?"

"Fuckin' A, I can." I could probably levitate right now with the way my body's buzzing.

"Let me see," she says.

In this moment, with this girl below me, I don't think I've ever had a better night.

CHAPTER 9
BIANCA

"LIKE THIS?" He grips the back of my neck with just enough pressure to send tingles down my spine.

I felt tiny standing next to Vinnie, but with him on top of me, holding me in his arms, I feel even smaller and even more turned on.

"Just like that." My voice cracks a little, which has Vinnie smirking. "Now, can you move?"

"Move?" He raises an eyebrow with a smirk.

He's playing dumb, but he knows exactly where I'm going with this. He just wants to hear me say the words.

"Yeah, like could you fuck me in this position?"

"Baby." His smirk turns into a wide smile. "I could fuck you in any position."

My mouth is suddenly dry, and no amount of swallowing helps. I need to remember we're working and he's helping me with a problem. We're not actually going to do it. "Can you be serious for a minute? This is important."

"Can you let yourself be free and spontaneous for a hot second?"

I used to be more spontaneous, but the older I get and the more pressure that comes along with my work, I find it hard to let myself be so frivolous. Especially as a deadline approaches, my entire life becomes about work and word count. It's something most men can't deal with. No one likes to play second fiddle to my computer.

"Do you want to help me with the book or not?"

"I'm here, aren't I?"

I slide my arms around his shoulders and bury my fingers in the back of his brown hair. "Try to move."

He stares down at me, still holding his crotch far away from me. "I'm going to be real honest here, Bianca. I'm super turned on, and I don't want you to slap me in the face if my cock touches you."

"I promise not to slap you. It's just a cock."

"It's not just a cock. It's my cock, which is currently hard, and I'm worried if I touch you with it, you might not actually get any work done tonight."

"We'll be fine," I tell him, but I'm not entirely convinced. After six months, my body's craving to be filled, and with the way Vinnie's looking at me, I can feel my willpower slipping. "We're adults and professionals, right? It's not like you have a magical cock."

"I'm always a professional." He's hovering above me, looking sexy as hell with the way he's staring down at me. "And it is indeed magical as fuck."

This may be my dumbest idea yet, but I needed his help because this worked in my head, but my editor disagreed.

He lowers his body on top of mine, settling between my legs. "Is this okay?" he asks.

I finally feel what he's packing, and my pussy contracts, loving the hardness of his cock pressing against me. "It's perfect."

"Uncomfortable?" he asks.

"No," I say, but my voice changes when I speak those words. A need I haven't felt in so long overtakes me. "Give me a few thrusts."

He grips my ass harder, and he tightens his fingers around the back of my neck as he adjusts his body, sliding his cock against my sweat pants.

I bite my bottom lip, stopping myself from crying out in pleasure. It's like being back in high school, where the slightest touch puts my entire body into overdrive. I need to get a grip and quick.

I wrap my legs around his body, resting my feet slightly above his ass just like the heroine in my book. He moves his hips backward, his hardness leaving me for a moment before he thrusts forward, hitting my clit in exactly the right way. This time, I can't help but let out a little noise. A sexy smile spreads across his face. Any hope I had that he didn't hear the sound goes right out the window. I'm momentarily mortified and horny as hell too.

"This doesn't work for me," he says. "The position is

too clunky, and I can't move the way I'd want to if we were having sex."

I want to argue, telling him the position very much works for me, but I don't.

"Why not?" I ask.

"I can't get the right amount of thrust from my legs alone, and my arms aren't useful in this position."

The right amount of thrust? It felt pretty damn good to me. Maybe I've been sexless for far too long and forgot what a good fucking entailed.

He moves his body backward, taking me with him, still holding my ass and my neck in his hands. We're suddenly upright, face-to-face, my core against his cock as I sit in his lap.

"This would be better."

I nod, unable to speak. His mouth is so close to mine, his warm breath moving across my face, almost caressing my skin.

"Yes, this is much better," he murmurs. He digs his fingers into my ass, pulling me closer, leaving no space between our bodies.

My heart races uncontrollably as my skin buzzes from the contact. "Why is it better?" I whisper, memorizing the way his body feels under me.

The thickness of his cock.

The smell of his skin.

The way his hands touch me.

Later, when he finally leaves, I'll be using every memory to take care of my "situation."

"In this position, I can kiss you," he says, staring into my eyes. "You can ride my cock, but I'd control the speed with my hand and can thrust upward for a little more impact." He squeezes my ass and presses his cock into me a little harder.

I suck in a breath, trying not to be affected by the way he's touching me and the hungry look in his eyes, but Jesus Christ...I want him.

He slides his fingers up my neck, tangling them in my hair with just the right amount of delicious bite. "This is the position I'd use. I could look at your beautiful face, kiss you hard, fuck you deep, and control your every movement for my pleasure."

"You'd control me?" I squeak out because his cock is making it damn near impossible for me to think, let alone speak like a normal human being.

He moves his lips closer, and all the air I had in my lungs vanishes. "Want me to show you? With our clothes on, of course."

I nod, but I know this is dangerous territory. Everything that's happened in the last few minutes has me hanging off the edge of my self-induced celibacy.

"I'm going to kiss you. We need this to be authentic."

I don't say no. Who would? Not a girl who hasn't been touched in months. Not a woman who's spent days upon days writing spicy sex scenes and the last few hours daydreaming of her sexy neighbor. The very one who's now under me, holding me in his arms.

The air in the room seems to vanish while I lose myself in his dreamy eyes as he leans closer. My heart hammers in my chest, and my entire body is on fire, craving his lips more than anything.

He tilts my head and brings my face closer.

"Is this a good idea?" I whisper as I dip my eyes to his lush lips, almost begging for his mouth.

"I want nothing more than to kiss you, Bianca. I haven't been able to think about much else."

The hairs on the back of my neck stand as he presses his lips to mine. I can't hold back the moan that's been sitting on the tip of my tongue since the moment I felt his body against mine.

His lips are just as velvety soft as I imagined—the exact opposite of the rest of his rock-hard body. I dig my nails into his scalp as I sweep my tongue across his lips, wanting more and needing to taste him.

"Baby," he murmurs. "I want you so bad."

"I want you too," I whisper into his mouth before he deepens the kiss, stopping me from saying more.

I feel Vinnie all over. My neck. My ass. My pussy. Our tongues tangle together as he moves my middle against his cock, dry-humping me.

My mind is everywhere and nowhere all at once. I can't think about anything but the way he's touching me, kissing me, and fucking me through my sweat pants.

I rock into him, wanting more of his delicious hardness against my clit and needing to come more than anything in the world.

Our bodies are moving torturously slow as I ride him. His hand slides from my ass to my waist, controlling my movements and the speed. He kisses me harder than before as his cock presses against my clit so perfectly, I nearly come.

I gasp with the next pass of his swollen cock over my clit, so close to the edge, my toes start to curl. The orgasm builds inside me, threatening to explode.

Vinnie moans, rocking into me, matching my movements. I want to look into his eyes, see his face, but I don't dare. I'm too lost in pleasure as the friction from his dick and my sweat pants drives me closer to the edge.

"I'm going to come," I whisper against his lips, gasping for air and knowing this is the last chance I have to stop what's about to happen.

"Let go, baby. Give in," he tells me. "Come on my cock."

The way he talks to me causes my insides to convulse and a massive orgasm to crash down on me so hard, I can't breathe. He tightens his hand on my neck, pulling me down harder against his body as he fucks me through my pants.

My body quakes uncontrollably, almost bucking as the orgasm rips through my system at record speed. He grunts, gasping for air, following me into bliss.

I don't know what happened. How in the hell did I come from dry-humping? My last few boyfriends couldn't get me off even after trying and pulling out all the stops. I'd always have to reach into my nightstand and grab my vibrator to finish the job.

The kiss slows as the only sounds in the room are our ragged breathing and pounding hearts.

"Fuck," he mutters, resting his forehead against mine. "That was…"

I want to say so many words.

Hot.

Awkward.

Embarrassing.

Unforgettable.

"Yeah," I reply instead, still unable to open my eyes and look at the man I just dry-humped until I came.

I don't know how long we sit like this. Me in his lap, my sweat pants soaked and my body trembling, before he finally speaks again.

He drops his hand from my neck to the middle of my back. "I'm sorry."

"For what?" I whisper, trying to take deep breaths and calm my racing, post-orgasm heart.

"I was supposed to be helping you, and I think I just made everything more complicated."

Complicated doesn't even begin to describe everything I'm feeling in this moment. I don't think any of my boyfriends have ever made me come, not even after giving it a valiant effort with their cocks, hands, or tongues. But then along comes Vinnie Gallo, football superstar, and he gets me off without even removing a piece of clothing.

"This has never happened to me," he admits.

I finally open my eyes and look at him. "What?"

"I've never come like this. I usually have more stamina, but I couldn't stop. The little noises you make made it impossible for me not to come. That was hot as fuck."

"It was."

"And when you came, the way you moaned as you rode my cock... Baby, that was the sexiest thing I've ever experienced."

My face heats. "Don't talk," I tell him and cover his mouth with my hand, still unable to look him in the eye.

Talking about coming in my sweat pants in front of a man I barely know is a little out of my comfort zone.

He pulls his face back a little, and my embarrassment grows. "Don't be ashamed. It's not like you came by yourself."

"We weren't supposed to..." I trail off, unsure what to call what just happened.

"Your position didn't work. We had to explore all avenues and, honestly," he says, running the backs of his fingers down my cheek. "I wouldn't want anyone else in my place. I want to be your go-to book research guy."

I push off him, slowly climbing to my feet and praying my legs don't give out. "I don't think that's a good idea."

His eyebrows pull down in the middle. "Why not?"

My eyes dip to the very wet spot on the front of his

sweat pants, a mix of my orgasm and his. "This is dangerous."

He smiles and slowly shakes his head. "This isn't dangerous, Bianca." He stands, closing the space between us and reaching out to run a finger down the side of my throat. "This is sexy. You have a book to finish, yeah?"

I nod and swallow, knowing he's going to try to sell me on being my real-life sex doll. I also know there's no way I can turn him down. Not after the way he kissed me and the head-spinning orgasm he delivered without even trying.

"Did this help you finish the scene?"

I nod again.

"Then we've accomplished something amazing. I can't wait to read what you write."

I stare at him, wide-eyed, imagining him reading the dirty words as he sits alone in his apartment. Will he touch himself and think of me?

I shake my head, trying to get rid of the image of him with his hard cock in his giant hands, stroking himself off as he reads. "I better get back to work," I tell him, needing to put space between us because this is all kinds of wrong.

"I'll let you get to it. Send me the chapter when you're finished." He stands up, and his cock is still clearly visible behind the wet spot.

"I can't. I don't share my work with anyone until I've finished the entire book."

"Just this chapter. Please," he begs.

My resistance slips because he's looking at me with those hungry eyes and those lips so close, I could almost kiss him again. "Okay," I say, like an idiot.

His lips touch mine for only a moment, soft and gentle, and then he's gone.

I'm left standing in my living room, staring at the door, wondering what in the hell just happened.

CHAPTER 10
VINNIE

"HOW'S THAT hot mama of yours?" Clarence asks as I gather up a few things from my locker before I head home.

Tonight's the night I meet Bianca's entire family, and I'm nervous as fuck.

"She's great, man. Busy writing, so I haven't seen her much."

"Is the sex as wild as I think it is? I mean, if my woman wrote those books—" he grabs his junk underneath his towel "—I'm sure she'd practically be hanging off my cock like it was a jungle gym."

"Can't keep her off me," I lie.

I haven't heard from her since the other night after she came apart in my arms and I exploded in my pants. I don't know what came over me or how the friction from the sweat pants combined with the tiny sounds she makes when being pleasured were enough to make me come like a virginal teenage boy.

"Lucky bastard." Clarence punches my shoulder.

"I'm meeting her family tonight." My stomach turns at the very thought.

I haven't met any girl's parents since I was in high school. I never stuck around long enough in college to make it even a remote possibility. Although Bianca and I entered into this together as a mutual agreement, it's feeling more real than fake.

"They fans?"

I nod. "Huge fans."

"Then you're solid. You can do no wrong."

I can think of plenty of things I can do wrong.

"Is that what it was like when you met Marquita's parents?"

He shakes his head. "Hell no. They hated me. I was a punk college player, and they didn't see a future for their princess with a nobody like me."

"And now?"

"Now they kiss my ass." He laughs. "They brag to all their snobby friends about their rich, successful son-in-law. It's quite a change from the way they used to describe me. Even after all these years, I've never forgotten the way they treated me."

Marquita isn't much different from her parents. Clarence doesn't see it, but she's a total snob. She looks down her nose at everyone, but I'm not the one who has to sleep with her.

"That's pretty shitty. Sorry you had to go through that."

"You're good, though. Bianca's family will love you.

What's not to like? Pretty face, local football hero, rich as fuck."

"Not exactly how some people see me."

Clarence looks at me funny. "No one looks at you any other way, dumbass. You hit the jackpot and all the stars aligned when your ass was born."

"Yeah," I mumble.

If the jackpot was a mafia boss father who spent more time behind bars than raising me, then I hit the big one. I know I've been lucky. How many kids dream of playing professional football and actually do it? Not that fucking many.

"I'd better go so I'm not late. Bianca will have my balls."

"Good luck, man. Knock 'em dead tonight. You got this."

I'm halfway down the hallway when Tracie comes around a corner like she'd been waiting for me. "There you are," she says, sliding her hand up my sweaty T-shirt, looking at me like I'm a piece of meat and she's starving for a bite. "I've missed you."

I peel her hand away from my chest and grip her wrist tighter than I have before. "Don't touch me."

She pouts like it's going to have any effect on me. "Don't be that way, silly."

"Gallo," Coach Malik says from behind me. "Go on ahead. I need to talk to Tracie."

I drop her hand and glare at her. "Leave me alone, Tracie. It's the last warning I'm going to give you."

"It's that bitch, isn't it?"

My body stiffens, and an anger I haven't felt in years courses through my veins. My hands ball up at my sides, and I'm about to open my mouth when Coach puts his hand on my shoulder, stopping me.

"Go, Vinnie. Don't do anything stupid. Let me talk with her."

I don't turn around.

I don't speak.

I walk off, leaving Tracie and the coach to hash out the shit she's still pulling with me, even after warnings from her grandfather.

"Whoa." It's the only word that comes to mind when Bianca opens the door to her place.

She's dressed in a cream-colored gown, covered with lace and so many frills, she looks more like a princess than a writer. She grabs the bottom, holding it out and showing me all the layers. "It's not too much?"

"You look…" I trail off and step forward, running my hand up her arm. "…like the most beautiful girl in the world."

She doesn't move away from my touch. "You're looking quite handsome yourself, but then again, you clean up well."

"Says the girl who pulls off sweat pants and a messy bun."

She rolls her eyes. "Now I know you're lying. I, in no way, pull off or look good in my writing outfit."

"Baby." I slide my hand up her arm before I trace her exposed collarbone with my finger. "You, wearing that outfit, riding me and moaning my name... There has never been anything sexier."

"Vinnie." She looks at me with those big brown eyes. "Don't. We can't miss this party."

"Don't what?" I play innocent, but all I want to do is walk her backward, peel off that dress, and bury my head between her legs. I've been dying to know what she tastes like, how different she'll sound coming on my tongue instead of through her pants.

"You're trying to seduce me."

"Is it working?" I raise an eyebrow, hoping like fuck she says yes.

"Not one bit." She smiles coyly, and I know she's lying. "We can't be late, or my parents will kill me."

"Well, my chariot awaits."

She shakes her head. "I'm driving. This is my night, and I'm not squeezing all these layers inside that tiny sports car of yours."

I like when she's bossy. "Whatever makes you happy."

She tries to walk in front of me as we make our way toward the elevator, but I pull her backward, wanting her at my side.

"You don't have to pretend yet. We're alone," she says as she pushes the button on the wall, but she doesn't look at me as she speaks.

"Who's pretending?" I stare at her, waiting for her to look at me. "I'm not."

I don't know what she isn't getting. Maybe I haven't made myself clear. I know we started this as some arrangement to help each other out, scratch each other's backs, but that's not how things have evolved this week.

"You don't have to do this." She stares down at the marble floor. "After tonight, you never have to see me again."

I turn her to face me and place two fingers under her chin, forcing her to look at me. "Baby, don't say those words. This may have started out as a favor, but there's nowhere I'd rather be tonight than at your side. Don't you know that?"

I've never had a chick push me away as many times as Bianca. Usually, I'm the one backtracking, trying to get them to move on and realize there's no future. I don't know what's ahead for Bianca and me, but I want to ride this as long as I can and figure shit out.

She parts her lips, and it takes everything in me not to kiss her. "You want to date me?" She blinks a few times, probably just as shocked by that admission as I am.

"I want to see where whatever this is takes us."

"Let's see if we survive tonight, and we'll talk."

She didn't say no, but she's making me more nervous about tonight than I already was.

"Are they going to hate me?" I ask, trying to swallow down the nerves that have been climbing up my throat.

"My brothers will both like and hate you. I'm their

little sister, and they're protective. The rest of my family might not be overly thrilled that I'm not dating a Latino guy."

"I can't change who I am. I'm sure they'll love me anyway. I mean, look at me, what's not to like?"

She laughs and slaps my chest playfully. "You're okay for a white boy. At least my mother will stop trying to fix me up with every available man she knows."

Her mother sounds like mine, always sticking her nose where it doesn't belong. I have one mission tonight. Win over Bianca's family. It's the only way there's any hope of moving beyond our dry-humping on her couch.

"I'll make them happy I'm yours." I usher her into the elevator as soon as the doors open.

She inhales slowly and plasters her back against the wall. "My family isn't going to be as easy to convince as your team, Vinnie." She closes her eyes, resting her head against the wood wall. "I haven't had a real boyfriend in a while, and if we're not careful, they'll see right through the lie."

"We're lying?"

"We are." She nods.

"You're attracted to me?" I ask, touching her hips as I face her.

"I am."

"I'm so attracted to you, Bianca. It's taking all my willpower not to kiss you right now and fuck you right here."

She sucks in a quick breath.

"I know what you look like when you come. I know the tiny noises you make as you rock against my cock. I'm pretty sure I know enough to make it believable."

"I wouldn't announce that to my family."

"I'm not an idiot, and anything I do tonight will be real and genuine. I'm done playing, baby."

"Vinnie, I can't make a commitment. Not now."

"You will," I tell her. "After tonight, you're going to be begging to be my girl."

That's the one thing I'm sure of. I'll do everything in my power to win over this girl and make her mine. The realization hits me square in the chest, stealing my breath like I was just sucker-punched.

I've never felt this way before, and it scares the shit out of me.

CHAPTER 11
BIANCA

"I THOUGHT you said this was a small anniversary party." Vinnie has his hand on my lower back, guiding me through the lobby toward the ballroom.

The music's so loud, the vases lining the hallways are vibrating against the tables, creating music of their own.

"I never said small." I hold in my laughter. The Hernandez family doesn't know what the word small even means. From cooking to parties, everything is big.

"This is a wedding, baby."

I shake my head. "It's my parents' thirtieth wedding anniversary, silly. Doesn't your family do this?"

He shakes his head as we continue walking toward the packed ballroom. "My parents just got married a few months ago."

I blink in confusion. "What?"

"It's a long story."

"Bianca," my brother Luis says as soon as he sees us walk into the ballroom.

It's like he was waiting at the entrance for us, trying to get his first look at the new man on my arm. I'm pretty sure he wanted to put the fear of God into whoever is dating his little sister, but I have a trick up my sleeve with the hot footballer my brother can't help but love.

With my past boyfriends, and I use that term loosely, it was pretty easy for my brothers to intimidate them. The guys were always scrawny, nerdy types who probably couldn't throw a punch to save their life—or my own. But Vinnie...he is the entire package and the perfect complement to my brothers' sizes and attitudes.

"Luis." I smile, finally happy with who's standing behind me.

It's a game my brothers play with the men in my life. It's a wicked game of cat and mouse, putting the fear of God in them if any harm, including sex, comes to me. They're lame. Always have been. From the day I first started getting boobs, it became their personal mission to keep me safe and my virtue intact.

Luis's not looking at me; he's glaring at Vinnie like I don't even exist anymore. Watching the two of them posturing is like watching an episode of exotic animal behavior on National Geographic.

I place my hand on Vinnie's chest and curl into his side, just to see my brother's body puff up with anger. "This is Vinnie. My boyfriend." I drive the second sentence home when I pop up on my tiptoes and plant a big, wet kiss on Vinnie's lips.

Vinnie's hand goes to my waist, digging his fingertips into my skin through all the layers of lace. "What are you doing, baby? Trying to get me killed?" he whispers with a small smirk.

"What's going on over here?" Right on cue, Javier makes his appearance.

I back away from Vinnie, smiling up at him. "Javi, this is Vinnie."

"Her boyfriend," Luis tells him, waving his arm in our direction as I swing around to face them both. "If you can't already tell by the way he's sucking our sister's face."

I roll my eyes because these two could turn the smallest act of affection into banging in public.

"I see that." Javi runs his hands through his hair like he's debating if he should make a scene or not.

He's done it before. Hell, they both have.

Vinnie puts his hand out, thinking maybe if he introduces himself, my brothers will somehow chill out. "I'm Vinnie," he says to Javi like my brother's instantly going to turn into someone other than an asshole because Vinnie extended his hand to him.

They both stare at him, shoulders squared, and the tiny vein they both have in their foreheads starts to protrude like it's ready to pop.

"Vinnie Gallo," I add with a smirk. "Maybe you've heard of him? He just got signed by your favorite football team."

They rock backward on their heels, acting more like clones than two separate people as the realization of who Vinnie actually is hits them square in the chest.

"The rookie quarterback for Chicago?" Luis asks, like he's not quite believing what I just said.

Vinnie smiles with a quick nod. "The one and only."

"No shit." Javi's face softens, and for a moment, I'm hopeful my brothers will finally play nice with one of my dates.

"The notorious womanizer," Luis adds like he knows everything there is to know about Vinnie.

Javi crosses his arms in front of his chest, and the hard stare he had earlier is back. "You have quite the reputation."

"It's all lies. I'm dedicated and faithful to your sister. Look at her." Vinnie dips his head to me. "She's a knockout and smart, too."

"I don't like this," Luis says because he's never been one to bite his tongue.

"A professional football player isn't the right match for you," Javi agrees with Luis, telling me who I should date, as if their opinions matter.

I want to knee them both in the junk. Instead, I slide my hand underneath the back of Vinnie's suit jacket, loving the dip of his muscles near the center of his back. "Can you give me a minute with my brothers?"

"Sure, baby. Want a drink?"

"I'd love something stiff, sweetheart." I smile when both of my brothers grunt their disapproval of the word I used, which I totally did on purpose.

"Anything you want. I'll be back in a minute."

I stare at my two brothers, none of us saying anything until Vinnie's a few feet away. I place my hands on my hips and glare at my brothers for being such enormous assholes. "You two need to stop right now. I like him. He's been nothing but an absolute gentleman to me."

If you don't count dry-humping me on the couch the other night, but I leave that part out.

"Football players are dogs, Bianca," Luis says.

"All men are, Luis. You, yourself, are a total womanizer, and you don't hear me trying to run off every woman you bring around."

Luis crosses his arms, not backing down, and I can tell this isn't going to be as easy as I thought. "You're my sister. It's my job to protect you."

"It was your job to protect me when I was little. I'm twenty-five now. I can defend myself. And you—" I point at Javi, waving my finger. "I expected more from you."

Javi throws his arms out. "I didn't do anything."

"You're jumping on the Luis bandwagon. So help me God, if you two try to chase Vinnie away, I'll elope with him as payback."

Luis's eyes widen. "You wouldn't."

I smirk. "Try me."

Luis runs his hand through his dark hair and glances down at the floor. "We just don't want to see you hurt, Bianca."

"I'm happy for the first time in a long time. I just

want you two to be supportive and not try to run him off. He doesn't scare easily like the other guys."

"Well, yeah. He's a man." Luis laughs, jabbing my brother in the ribs. "Not a pussy like the other guys."

"Then be happy for me, or I'll make you both sorry."

My brothers remain silent as Vinnie returns with two drinks in his hands. I take my drink, whatever it is, and drink half the glass before Vinnie says his next words.

"I'd love it if you guys came to a game this season, or you could come by practice and watch the team work out."

That's all he had to say to two die-hard football fans. Between my talk and Vinnie's bribe, they finally chill the fuck out.

"That would be great, man," Javi says, almost cracking a smile.

"We wouldn't want to impose," Luis adds, but he's completely full of shit.

"I insist that you come as my personal guests." Vinnie tips his head, impressing me with his ability to think on his feet and not being the least bit fazed by my brothers.

I wrap my arm around Vinnie's back, practically plastering myself against him just because I know it's going to piss off Luis and Javier. "Now if you'll excuse us, we're going to see Mom and Dad."

They don't say a word, only grunt, the closest thing they can do without me losing my shit on them.

"Sorry they're assholes," I tell Vinnie as we head

toward the reception line near the steps to the dance floor.

His arm is around my back, gripping my hip with his massive hand. "They're your brothers. It's their job to be assholes, Bianca. I'd be worried if they weren't."

"My parents will be easier. My mother will be happy I'm not alone."

He glances down at me as we get closer. "And your father?"

"He wants whatever makes me happy, and he's your biggest fan."

My father's eyes light up as soon as he sees me. That's the way it always is with him. He says I'm his greatest joy. I can literally do no wrong in my father's eyes. My mother is a little tougher, worried I'll grow old and be alone forever.

"*Mija*," my father says, holding out his arms to me.

I release Vinnie and walk into my father's embrace, wrapping my arms around him tightly. "Hi, Papa."

"I've missed you," he whispers in my ear. "You're always locked away in that apartment of yours, typing away on your keyboard."

"I'm on a deadline. I'm sorry."

He backs away and cups my face. "Don't ever be sorry for following your dream. I'm so proud of you."

My insides warm at his words. "Thanks, Papa."

My father's eyes finally leave me, catching sight of the handsome man standing behind me. "Who do we have here?"

I reach out, hooking my arm through Vinnie's. "This is my boyfriend, Vinnie."

Vinnie holds out his hand. "It's an honor to meet you, sir."

"You look familiar, son. Where do I know you from?"

"Papa, this is Vinnie Gallo. He plays football for Chicago."

My father slides his hand into Vinnie's palm. "The superstar?"

Vinnie's smile grows, and he stands a little taller. "Some people say that."

My father looks at me, his hand still shaking Vinnie's. "You're dating a professional football player?"

I nod, unable to wipe the proud smile off my face. "Yes, Papa. He's also my neighbor."

"Oh my word," my mother finally says after an aunt once removed and someone I've only seen once in my life finally walks away, letting her come up for air. "That woman can talk." My mother roams her eyes over Vinnie, soaking in his handsome face, wide shoulders, and all-around huge, muscular body.

"Mama, this is Vinnie."

"The boyfriend?" my mother asks, still staring at him like a piece of steak.

"Yes, ma'am," Vinnie answers with that smile that could have just about any girl dropping her panties and begging to be fucked.

My mother wiggles her fingers, motioning for Vinnie to come closer. "Let me get a better look at you."

Vinnie looks at me like I'm going to rescue him or give him permission, but I give him a little push in her direction. She's the entire reason I asked Vinnie to come with me to this party. Maybe now she'll get off my back and stop trying to fix me up with every available man she knows.

She touches his face first. "Well, aren't you handsome."

Vinnie smiles nervously, and it's totally adorable. "You're very beautiful yourself, Mrs. Hernandez."

She slides her hands down his thick neck to his shoulders. "Solid frame. Good genes. You'll make wonderful grandchildren."

Vinnie stiffens. "I don't think we're ready to have children yet," he tells her, letting her feel him up like she's buying livestock.

"I didn't plan to have Luis when I did either. Accidents happen, handsome."

I bite my lip to stop myself from laughing because I'm pretty sure Vinnie's going to be running for the hills by the time this evening is over. I haven't met his family, but they can't be as crazy as mine.

"My daughter will not have a child out of wedlock," my papa adds, still thinking of me as his virginal daughter, even though my books are as dirty as they come.

My mother eyes my father. "I remember my father saying the same words to you." She smirks and finally releases her hold on Vinnie.

"I made an honest woman out of you, Luciana," my

father says as he pulls my mother into his arms and presses his lips against hers.

So far, this evening is going exactly how I planned. My parents like Vinnie, and my brothers don't. But one thing's for sure; I'm no longer the lonely girl in their eyes, destined to be single forever.

"Your grandmother is waiting for you, Bianca," Mama says, glancing toward a table near the dance floor. "She's excited to meet Vinnie."

"Okay," I say with trepidation because my grandmother is like a human lie detector. If she doesn't give her blessing, we are doomed. "We'll be back."

"Should I be worried?" Vinnie asks as we make our way down the staircase.

"Put on your game face, Gallo. My grandmother is a tough one, and she'll see through any lie."

"What's to lie about, baby?"

He keeps calling me that, and I do nothing to correct him. Every romance novel I read where the man repeatedly calls the woman baby has me rolling my eyes so hard, I almost make myself dizzy. But for some reason, when he calls me baby, it makes my insides all warm and my belly flutter uncontrollably.

I stop on the bottom step and turn to face him. "If she doesn't think we're in love, she'll never give her blessing. She has a weird sixth sense about these types of things."

"I got you," he says with absolutely no hesitation.

I have no doubt he very much has me, and that's not something that's easy for me to admit.

CHAPTER 12
VINNIE

"COME CLOSER," her grandmother says, holding out her hands as we stand a few feet away. "I don't see so well anymore."

I don't know how old the woman is, but her face is weathered like she's spent most of her life in the sun. There are hints of Bianca's much younger features in the woman's face. The big, dark eyes, high cheekbones, and a small, delicate nose.

Bianca tightens her grip on my hand as I take a step forward, and I give her a little squeeze, letting her know it's okay. I've taken on way more formidable opponents than the tiny, frail woman in front of me.

"Down a little," the woman says, wiggling her fingers and motioning for me to leave almost no space between us.

"Oh lordy," Bianca whispers from behind me.

I glance over my shoulder with a wink and take a

knee in front of her grandmother's legs, releasing Bianca's hand.

The woman places her hands on my shoulders, working her fingertips into my muscles. "Strong shoulders." Her hands slide down my biceps, and there's a hint of a smile on her lips. "Big arms."

"Yes, ma'am." I smile, knowing this woman is feeling me up, but I'm okay with it because it's Bianca's grandmother.

"What do you do, boy?"

Bianca moves closer, casting a shadow over me. "His name is Vinnie, *Abuela*."

Her hands are on my forearms now, kneading my muscles through my suit jacket. "Do you work with your hands?" she asks as she moves her face closer, trying to see my features.

"In a way."

"A farmer?" she asks, being more direct.

"No, ma'am. I play football."

She turns my hands over, feeling my palms with two fingers. "Strong hands." She smiles. "Come closer. I want to see your face, and my old eyes fail me in this light."

I move forward until my chest presses against her knees, and I raise my face to hers. She cups my cheeks in her hands as she leans forward, almost touching noses with me. "You're the green-eyed one."

Word must spread fast in this family, or maybe Bianca's talked about me with her grandmother. Lord knows, in my family, if Betty knows something, the entire world has the information because the woman is shit at keeping secrets.

"I am." I can't wipe the dumb smile off my face knowing someone's been talking to her grandmother about me.

"I knew you'd come," she whispers as her fingertips slide to my mouth, outlining the edges of my lips. "The ancestors told me about you."

I don't move. *Ancestors?* Either her age has affected her brain, or she's talking to spirits. One makes me sad, and the other scares the shit out of me.

When I was fourteen, my friends dared me to go into this tiny mystic shop a couple streets over from the bar. Me being the man, of course, I walked in there without a problem. My head held high, shoulders back, thinking that shit was going to be a breeze and I'd end up with a few laughs. Just like any teenage punk who wanders into a place like that.

Until Bianca's abuela, I hadn't thought about the words that woman spoke to me almost a decade ago.

"You will fall madly in love with the brown-eyed girl next door."

Then, I was pretty sure Margaret Alfonsi was not going to be the future Mrs. Vincent Gallo. She was barely five feet tall but so skinny, her kneecaps looked like weapons. She had buck teeth, which could be adorable on some people, just not her. But the real issue with Margaret wasn't her face or body—it was her shitty attitude. She was the meanest girl on the street. She had to be, with the way the other kids picked on her. If you said anything to Margaret that seemed even remotely unfriendly, she'd hit you straight in the balls with those bony-ass kneecaps of hers.

"Abuela, don't scare him." Bianca places her hand on my shoulder and moves to my side.

I peer up at her with the hint of a smile and cover her hand with mine. "I'm fine, baby, let her speak."

"You care for my Bianca?" She pulls my face closer before dropping her hands back to my shoulders.

"I do."

"She's a headstrong and stubborn girl. Much like her abuela."

I laugh softly. Grandma isn't lying. Bianca has both those qualities, but I couldn't imagine her any other way. A weak woman isn't what I'm after. I want someone who's going to challenge me, and so far, Bianca's done that at every turn.

"She will need a firm hand and caring heart to watch over her."

"I can do that."

"*Mi amor* was my rock, holding me in place and keeping me tethered to this earth. You must be that for Bianca."

But for some odd reason, which is totally fucked up, my mind goes straight to sex. Holding Bianca in place as she rides my cock from above. And the firm hand part? Yeah, I'm totally thinking about smacking that ass.

I shake my head when Bianca smacks my shoulder like she can read my damn mind. "Vinnie," she whispers. "Don't go there."

Yeah. She totally read my mind. Of course, she would. She writes the dirtiest words about women being controlled and sexually dominated. There's no way her mind didn't shift a little with the firm hand comment.

"Yes," her grandmother says and touches my face again, bringing my attention back to her and away from my dirty thoughts. "You will make a fine father to my great-grandchildren."

"Will we have a lot?" I'm totally buying into her ancestor talk, and I'm also indulging the woman.

Bianca's foot starts to tap like she's dancing behind me. I reach back, wrapping my hand around her ankle to stop her. She grunts, and her shadow looms a little large over me. "Ridiculous," she whispers, knowing her abuela can't hear her, but I totally can.

"Many children. Many, many children." Her lips turn up into a satisfied smile. "The family legacy will continue through you," she says with a tight squeeze of my shoulders.

"Abuela." Bianca leans over and kisses her grandmother's cheek. "We're being summoned by Luis. We'll be back, though."

I glance around the room, and Luis's not even looking in our direction. I guess the conversation about children and a future has Bianca on edge and looking for an escape route.

Abuela stares at Bianca. "Don't lie, dear. It's not very nice."

I laugh quietly as I climb to my feet, and Bianca

looks like a deer in headlights. Even though her grandmother can't see well, she knows when someone's bullshitting her, especially her granddaughter.

"I..." Bianca starts to say, but I figure I'll rescue her from this situation.

"Abuela, do you mind if I take Bianca to get a drink?" I ask, trying to get her the exit she wants and save face with her grandmother.

"I don't mind." She eases back into her chair and toys with the wedding ring she still wears on her finger. "Bring this old lady a tequila when you come back."

Bianca slides her hand into mine and pulls me toward the bar before I can say another word to her grandmother. "She's not totally with it," she tells me when we're only a few feet away.

"She's fine."

"No." Bianca shakes her head. "She's not. Didn't you hear the things she was saying?"

I stop walking and tug on her hand, making her body lurch backward and collide with my chest. "Baby." I wrap an arm around her middle, gazing at this beautiful and exasperating creature. "Sometimes, the oldest people among us speak the most truth."

She gawks at me, blinking repeatedly as she stills in my arms. "You don't honestly believe anything she just said, do you?"

I lean forward, burying my face in her neck. "About the ancestors or the babies?"

She tips her head back as my lips press into her skin. "Both," she says breathlessly, and I know I've got her.

I nibble the spot right near her shoulder blade because I know she makes the hottest sound when I touch her there. "I very much believe her words." My hand slides to her stomach, splaying across her dress. "I'd love nothing more than to see your belly big and carrying my babies."

As the words come out of my mouth, I regret them. There're no takebacks. No turning back time. I've never said those words.

Fuck, I've never even thought them about anyone.

Never.

Ever.

No fucking way.

I'm a player.

A baller.

A man without a tether and have been very much enjoying my easy lifestyle until Bianca.

Bianca stiffens, and the tiny moans she was making cease. "I need a drink," she says as she pushes out of my arms. "Maybe ten."

I follow behind her, this time not reaching for her but having a mild anxiety attack instead. How could I have been so stupid as to say I want my babies in her belly? Like, I'm not even dating the woman.

Hell, this was all supposed to be a trick to get her family off her back and my coach off mine. But somewhere in the last week, lines have blurred.

Maybe it's the fact that she's not that interested. Or at least, she pretends she isn't. When she was in my lap, riding me like we were buck naked, she was very much interested in everything I had to offer and could give.

"Two shots of tequila," she tells the bartender, holding up two fingers.

I rub the back of my neck, hoping we'll both get so drunk, the entire night will become a blur. "I'm not a huge tequila fan." I stand next to her, watching the bartender as he grabs the bottle.

She stares in my direction, but there's no happiness on her face. I don't see anger either, but I can't nail down the exact emotion because she's so good at hiding how she's feeling. "They aren't for you."

As soon as the bartender pours the first, Bianca has it in her hands and slams it down. She doesn't even wince as she plops the shot glass back on the bar. My stomach turns at the very thought of tequila. We're not friends anymore. I always end up on the floor or with some chick I'd never sleep with sober after I've had one too many shots of that shit.

I pull the empty glass away from Bianca after she points at it like she wants a refill. "Slow down."

"Slow down?" she asks, her chest heaving. "Slow down?" Her voice is louder now, and people around us are starting to stare.

"Shh, baby."

"Baby?" She grunts and reaches for the second shot.

I pull the glass from her hand and set it back on the bar. Wrapping my fingers around her upper arms, I pull her close and lower my voice. "Look me in the eye and tell me you haven't touched yourself while thinking of me."

She narrows her eyes, and she doesn't speak. She's breathing faster, but her eyes never leave mine.

I move my lips to her ear. "Tell me you haven't moaned my name while dreaming of my cock buried so deep inside your tight, needy pussy you can't breathe."

She turns her face, her mouth almost touching mine.

I lick my lips, and her eyes follow. "If I touched you right now, put my hand up that pretty little dress of yours, would you be wet for me?"

A blush creeps across her cheeks at my words, but I don't stop.

"I'm hard for you. So fucking hard. I ache to be inside you, Bianca."

CHAPTER 13
BIANCA

VINNIE HOLDS my hand as he stalks through the ballroom like a man possessed. I don't say anything as we walk, still processing everything he just said to me. My mind and body are too consumed by lust to think about much else. My six-month sex hiatus is blowing up in my face.

"In here." He pulls me inside the empty coat room before I can object.

What is it about this guy that has me acting so unlike myself? I've never had any problem resisting men. Then Vinnie Gallo happened. Six-plus feet of solid muscle, green eyes, and tanned skin and I'm ready to jump into bed with him with barely a moment's hesitation.

He locks the door and stalks toward me with hunger in his eyes. "I can't wait any longer."

I stand here like I'm helpless, playing with the hem of my dress. "This isn't a good idea," I whisper and try to swallow down the need that's building inside me. "We shouldn't."

He wraps his fingers around my chin. "Tell me you don't want me, and we'll stop." His green eyes bore into me, challenging me to lie.

God, I want him. I want him so fucking bad, my entire body is vibrating with need. I stare at him, unable to form words as my heart hammers in my chest like I'm running a marathon. Before I can say anything, his lips crash down on mine, sealing away any doubt I have left.

I place my fingers against his abdomen, feeling his muscles ripple and flex underneath his shirt. The kiss deepens, and for a moment, I can't breathe. He's literally rendered me breathless. Like something out of an old movie or one of my romance novels.

My knees weaken, but Vinnie wraps an arm around my waist, pulling me closer and keeping me upright.

I slide my hands around to his back, finding the deep ridges near his spine, and anchor myself to him. He grunts, and my pussy contracts from the sound and the way his tongue sweeps along mine. Like it needs to remind me of how immensely empty and lonely my mouth has been.

He digs his teeth into my bottom lip and tugs as he grips my ass, grinding against me. I moan, loving the way he feels against my body and how infinitely small I feel in his hands.

"Hands or mouth?" he asks against my lips.

I open my eyes, finding him staring at me with those

blazing green eyes, just as breathless as I am. "Both," I whisper, wanting everything he's willing to give.

He instantly drops to his knees with his hands sliding up my legs, pushing my dress up around my waist. I glance down, unable to take my eyes off him. A satisfied grin spreads across his face when I'm fully exposed.

"No panties, baby? You wanted my mouth on your beautiful pussy, didn't you?"

I bite my lip, trying to pull off the innocent look, but God…I wanted this more than anything. He's so close, I can feel his warm breath caressing my bare skin.

His tongue darts out, sweeping across his irresistibly full lips as he lifts my leg over his shoulder. I hold my breath, leaning back against the wall for support and praying I can stay upright. Besides grinding against his cock separated by two pairs of sweat pants, my body hasn't been touched by another person in so long, I know it's not going to take much to get me off.

"She wants me," he says as he brings his face closer to me like he's talking to my pussy. His gaze flicks up, and my breath hitches as the overhead light shines on his face, making his green eyes almost glow.

As his lips press against my skin, my body rocks backward and I move my hips toward him, begging for more. I feel my eyes roll back. I can't keep them open. The pleasure is too much and yet not enough.

"So wet for me," he murmurs against my skin before his tongue sweeps across my clit.

Every fiber in my body comes alive as my body jolts.

I forget everything else except this moment, his lips and tongue, and the orgasm I so badly crave. My fingers tangle in the hair on top of his head, holding him there, making sure he doesn't stop.

I rock into his face as he seals his lips around me. He grips my thigh as I try to balance on one leg when all I really want to do is climb on top of his shoulders and ride his face to ecstasy.

He strokes his fingers between my legs, front to back, sending an entirely new, magical sensation through my body.

"So wet," he says again like I don't know I'm practically dripping with need.

"Shh," I whisper in the darkened room, wanting his mouth busy with my body and not with words. "Don't talk."

"My baby's bossy."

I don't need to look down to know there's a smile on his face. I can feel his lips curve up against my sensitive skin. I don't correct him that I'm not *his baby*. I'll be whatever he wants me to be as long as he doesn't stop again.

A single finger rubs against my opening, circling the sensitive skin so slowly, I almost start to beg to be filled. Inch by inch, he pushes the tip inside me, torturing me. I moan as he pulls his finger back out a bit, crooking it inside and rubbing against my G-spot. I want more. I need more.

As if he can read my mind, he adds a second finger,

filling me so completely, my pussy contracts at the pleasure of being stuffed again.

His mouth works in perfect rhythm with his hand,
sucking, flicking, fucking my pussy and clit in just the
right way. I can't stop the orgasm from coming, when
all I want to do is extend the pleasure and bask in the
ecstasy only his body can deliver.

"Yes! Yes!" I ride his face and fingers like I'm a
cowboy at the rodeo. "Just like that," I cry out as my toes
curl uncontrollably. "I'm coming. Oh God, I'm coming."

Vinnie doesn't stop. He doesn't slow down. He
picks up the pace, thrusting his fingers deeper and
harder inside my pussy than he was before. Colors flash
in the darkness as my body stiffens and a wave of pleasure crashes over me, sucking all the air from my lungs.
Thankfully, his face is buried because the look on my
face is anything but pretty as my mouth hangs open,
and I gasp for air that won't come.

My entire body convulses, my pussy contracting
over and over again, milking his fingers and prolonging
the orgasm. Just when I think the orgasm is nearing the
end, Vinnie curls those luscious fingers inside me again,
rubbing my G-spot relentlessly until another tsunami of
pleasure bursts free.

I grip his hair tightly, keeping me upright as I gasp
for air and try to fill my lungs again. My body twitches.
The aftershocks of an orgasm I haven't felt in…well,
forever because no one gives oral like Vinnie, vibrate
through my system.

"Fuck," he says against my skin, fingers still deep inside.

I stand there, one foot on the floor, the other flung over his shoulder, unable to breathe and not speaking. Who can talk after something like that?

Sure as fuck not me.

Opening one eye, I glance down at his beautiful face, his lips glistening with my orgasm.

"You're so hot, baby. You needed that."

I don't argue because, hello...orgasm brain. He could say just about anything, and I'd agree with him. I am too busy riding out the aftereffects to care about anything or to even form a sentence.

He places two fingers on his tongue, sucking them between his lips. He moans as he licks my juices off his skin, closing his eyes as if he's savoring every drop.

"So sweet." He smiles. "So fucking sweet."

I'm dumbfounded and mute as he places my foot back on the floor and grips my sides, sliding his hands up my body as he stands. I just stand there and blink, staring at this beautiful man who gave me a world-rocking orgasm.

"You okay?" he asks as his eyes darken.

I nod.

"You sure?"

I nod again and start to kneel when he wraps his hands around my arms and hauls me upward. "No, baby. Not here."

I blink a few times and stare because I was going to return the favor. It's only fair.

"I needed you to relax, and now you're perfect."

My lips part like I'm going to say something, but again, nothing comes. He backs up, looking at my face before he trails his eyes down my body.

"You look so beautiful right now," he says as he straightens the bottom of my dress, but he keeps his eyes locked on me. "Pink cheeks with a sheen of sweat I put on your skin."

I'm pretty sure my pink cheeks just turned the brightest shade of red. The hunger in his eyes is still there from earlier, burning brighter than before he gave me the amazing orgasm.

"We'd better go back to the party," I say, finally finding my words. "I'm sure people are looking for us."

My mind is a mess of emotions. Sex does that. What started out as an exchange of personal favors has turned into two orgasms, awakening feelings inside me I thought I had long since buried.

Maybe it's the way he looks at me. Maybe it's the way his body gives mine pleasure. Whatever it is, Vinnie has me practically wrapped around his finger.

As we exit the coat room, I look around, seeing if anyone spots us. No one's looking, of course. They're too busy talking and celebrating my parents' anniversary to even notice we snuck away.

Vinnie wraps an arm around my waist, resting his hand on my hip as he ushers me through the ballroom. "Smile," he tells me, but I hadn't realized I wasn't.

I do as he says. As we approach my abuela's table,

her face lights up like she knows the secret we're keeping.

"Sit," she commands, motioning toward the two empty chairs next to her. The wrinkles around her eyes deepen. "Make an old woman happy."

Vinnie pulls out the chair closest to Abuela, and I sit down. His hands are on my shoulders as he leans forward and whispers, "I'll get us some drinks while you get yourself together."

I nod as I stare straight ahead, like I'm in some post-orgasmic trance. He's not even a few feet away when my abuela takes my hand in hers, giving it a little squeeze.

"It's scary at first when it happens, sweetheart. Don't let your head get in the way of what's meant to be."

"When what happens?"

She laughs softly. "When you start to fall."

"I'm not," I begin to argue, but she shushes me.

"I see the way that man looks at you and how you stare at him. I may be old and my eyes may be failing me, but some things, even the blindest person can see." She pats my hand. "Don't let fear stop you from happiness. Broken hearts just propel us down our destined path until our souls find where they're meant to be."

CHAPTER 14
VINNIE

"I'M ON MY WAY, Ma. I'm just running a few minutes late."

"Busy night last night?" she asks on the other end of the phone as I step into the hallway to lock my door.

Bianca's standing in front of her door with her back to me, but she glances over her shoulder for a moment.

"Hey, baby," I say, loving the way her yoga pants hug her every curve.

"Who are you talking to?" Ma asks, but I ignore her.

"Hey." She smiles and turns back around.

"Staying in today?" I'm totally checking out her ass, and it's banging in those pants.

She turns again, catching me checking out her ass. "I have a chapter to write today. I'm chained to the keyboard yet again." She sighs. "The words just aren't coming like they usually do."

"Vinnie, who are you talking to?" Ma asks again, but

this time, she's louder, almost yelling at me on the other end.

"My girl, Ma. Bianca. She's my neighbor."

Bianca blushes. "Don't tell her that," she whispers, but there's still a hint of a smile on her face as if she likes the way that sounded.

"Bring her to dinner."

"Ma, I don't think—" I start to say, but Ma cuts me off.

"We want to meet your girl. Bring her, Vinnie. No exceptions or excuses." Then she hangs up.

I pull the phone away from my ear and stare at the screen. My mother never hangs up on me. Never. Maybe on my brothers and sister, but not on her little boy and pride and joy.

Bianca turns to face me finally. "What's wrong?"

"She said I have to bring you to dinner, and then she hung up."

"I can't go. I'm a mess. I just worked out, and I'm gross."

I take a step toward her, moving my eyes down her body. "You're beautiful. Just like you were in the closet last night."

Her cheeks turn pink, and she glances down at the floor. "You have to stop telling people I'm your girl. You fulfilled your end of the deal."

I touch her chin, forcing her eyes to mine. I don't know what she doesn't understand about this, but bargain or no bargain, I want her. "Do you like me?"

She swallows hard, staring at me with those big brown eyes. "I do, but…"

"No buts. I like you, Bianca, and I already said you're my girl. I don't say those words easily or often. So, get in there and do whatever you have to do, but you're coming with me to family dinner."

"But my work…"

"It'll be there later. Maybe I'll even give you a little inspiration when we get back." I smirk.

I love helping her with her work, especially when it ends with her in my lap, riding me like I'm her favorite stud.

She eyes me for a second before sighing. "Meeting your parents is a big step. It's a little soon for that, Vinnie."

"I met your entire family last night."

She narrows her eyes because she knows I'm right and she's grasping at straws. I'm not leaving this hallway until she's at my side. There's no way I'll walk into my mother's without Bianca, because my mother would lose her shit. And a mad Betty isn't fun.

"I need ten minutes."

"Take as long as you want. I'll wait." I turn her body toward her door when she doesn't move, just stands there, blinking at me. "I'll just read while I wait."

She mumbles under her breath as she unlocks the door, but I can't make out exactly what she says. She drops her keys on the kitchen counter, still talking to herself, before she disappears into the bedroom.

I grab a book off the coffee table before relaxing into

her couch. The very place she came in my lap only a few days ago. The sounds and smells of that night come flooding back as I crack open the paperback somewhere in the middle to kill some time.

I read the first sentence on some random page, finishing the entire page quickly. I glance toward Bianca's bedroom before flipping the book closed, keeping my finger inside it to hold my page, and stare at the cover. The book looks innocent enough, but what's inside is anything but.

Is this what Bianca's into? Does she have some secret fantasy about being kidnapped and used? I think it's every man's fantasy. I don't know a guy alive who wouldn't mind being held captive and made to repeatedly fuck people until they orgasm. But never in a million fucking years did I think Bianca was into this kind of thing.

I open the book again and continue, wondering if the book should be turning me on as much as it is. I'm adjusting my cock, so totally immersed in the scene, I don't even hear Bianca walk back into the living room.

"What are you reading?" She tries to take the book from my hands, but I hold on tight.

I don't look up, just stare at the page, having to know how the scene ends. "Shush. It's getting good."

"Is it? I haven't read it yet. A friend sent it to me and said it was dark."

"Uh-huh. I feel dirty liking it."

She giggles and ruffles my hair. "Ah, it's a mindfuck book."

I tip my head back, staring up at her and seeing nothing but tits above my face, which does fuck-all to help the situation in my pants. "A what?"

"Something that fucks with your head. You know you shouldn't like it, but you do. And for that, you feel so dirty and wrong."

"I'm there, baby. So there. Take your time. But if you take too long, we're not making it out of the house without you putting your tits in my face while I read this book."

She giggles again, and my cock twitches, begging for something...anything. It takes all my resistance not to chase after her when she jiggles her tits above me before running back to her bedroom.

"Tease!" I yell out.

"Am not!"

She's not a tease, but fuck, the girl hasn't even laid a hand on my cock, let alone let me slide between her sweet thighs. She's had two amazing orgasms—whether or not she wants to admit to that, I know for sure it's true. While I had one in my pants just from the friction of her beautiful cunt and my sweat pants.

I can't stop turning the pages, my mouth hanging open. I don't know how much time passes before she steps back into the living room and clears her throat.

"I'm ready. Are we going?"

I hold up a finger, finishing the last words on the page. "One sec."

She pulls the book from my hand, and I groan, needing to know what's going to happen next. "Take the book home and finish it," she tells me with a smirk. "I didn't know you liked to read so much."

"Fuck. I didn't either." I motion for her to give the book back. "But I want to finish it and yours too."

"Is Vinnie Gallo a secret romance lover?"

"Shut your mouth. Don't you dare tell anyone."

She places her hands on her hips and smiles. "What do I get to keep my mouth shut?"

"All the orgasms you want." It's a win-win for me.

Her orgasms will probably lead to mine. At least, I hope to fuck, someday they will.

She moves her head from side to side like she has to think about what I'm offering as I stalk toward her. "That could work."

I pull her against me, letting her feel my cock that's begging for her. "Baby, you know you love the way I make you come, and I haven't even buried my cock so deep inside you that you can't breathe."

"I…"

"Shh." I place my finger against her lips. "Imagine the kind of pleasure I can deliver when using my entire arsenal. Let that sink in."

Her lips part behind my fingers, and she lets out a long, shaky breath with her eyes locked on mine. "We better go," she whispers.

"If my mother weren't waiting, I'd…" I can't even finish the sentence. It's too dirty, and my cock's too hard.

She shakes her head and closes her eyes. "Don't say it, or I won't want to leave."

From her lips to God's ears. I already don't want to leave, and it's my family we're going to see. I drop my eyes to her breasts. Even covered by a T-shirt, they're begging for my touch, my lips. "I want you tonight. I'm sick of waiting."

"I need to work," she reminds me, using it as an excuse.

"I'll be your inspiration. Call it research."

A small smile spreads across her face.

I've got this one in the bag. No one meets my family and doesn't fall immediately in love with them.

CHAPTER 15
BIANCA

"THIS IS MY BROTHER LUCIO, his wife Delilah, my sister Daphne, her husband Leo, my oldest brother Angelo, and his fiancée Tilly."

I stand in stunned silence as Vinnie points to each sibling and their respective partner as we stand in the living room. It's like I've walked into the twilight zone where everyone's beautiful and muscular. The genes in this family run deep and strong.

Vinnie pulls me closer. "This is my girl, Bianca."

I'm not the only one gawking. They're looking at me like I'm an act in a sideshow. I almost wonder if I have something on my face because their eyes are hard and fixed on me.

"You brought a girl to dinner?" Daphne, his sister, asks like she's in shock.

"Not just any girl, Daphne. *My* girl."

He keeps calling me that, along with baby. Over and over again, he drives the point home, even though we haven't had a conversation where we've solidified our relationship status.

Angelo nods slowly as a smile spreads across his face. "Never thought I'd see the day."

I lean over, their eyes still on me, and whisper in Vinnie's ear. "Why are they looking at me like that?"

He looks down with a small smirk and his hand firmly on my hip. "Because I never bring anyone to dinner."

"Never?"

Vinnie shakes his head.

"Why me?" I ask as my belly flips.

"Because, baby, I told you…" He pauses and ticks his head toward his siblings. "You're my girl."

He's already said that, but it doesn't help explain anything.

"We're happy to have you here, Bianca," Lucio says as he bounces a tiny baby in his arms. "It's not every day Vinnie brings home a girlfriend." Lucio makes a funny face as he says the last word, as if it's foreign on his tongue.

"It's never happened." Daphne steps around Lucio and Angelo and holds out her hand to me. "It's wonderful to meet you." Her eyes go to her brother. "It's nice to see my brother is settling down."

I know what she's saying without her actually saying the words. Vinnie's a player. I knew the type in high school and college. The big man on campus with so many girls fawning over him and vying for his attention it was bound to go to his head. I can't even fathom the number of women Vinnie's been with, and the very thought makes my stomach twist into a tight knot.

"Is Vinnie here?" a woman calls out from the next room.

"He is, and he brought a *girlfriend*!" Daphne yells back.

The woman runs out of the kitchen, wearing an apron and wielding a spatula like it's a sword, and she comes straight toward us. Her beautiful red hair bounces near her shoulders when she stops right in front of us. She grabs Vinnie's face, smashing his cheeks in her palms like he's a little kid. "Baby," she says and kisses his cheeks near her hands. "You look good." She studies him for a second, thankfully, ignoring me. "You look happy."

"I am, Ma," he says, but his words are garbled. "This is Bianca."

His mother releases her hold on him and takes a step back to look at me. Her eyes sweep from my face down and then back up. "Well, aren't you a looker." She smiles and moves closer. "High cheekbones, beautiful golden skin, hips perfect for baby-making."

I give Vinnie the side-eye. I've never had anyone describe my hips as perfect baby-makers. I'm not a twig, never have been and never will be. But baby-maker?

"Hi," I say nervously and fidget with my hands because I don't know what else to do.

His siblings are in shock that I'm here, and his

mother, much like my grandmother, already has us starting a family.

Awkward.

"You're absolutely stunning." His mother smiles before reaching out, handing Angelo the spatula and grabbing me into a bear hug. Vinnie's hands disappear from my hips, giving me over to his mother without hesitation.

"She's a writer, Ma," Vinnie says proudly. "A good one too."

She pulls her head back, looking at me in awe but still holding me so tightly, I can barely breathe. "A smart girl. Santino!" she yells over her shoulder. "Get your ass in here and meet Vinnie's girl." She smiles at me. "Sorry, he's watching the Sox in the den."

"Well, at least it's not the Cubs." I laugh.

A handsome older man, not as built as the younger ones, steps into the living room. He's mumbling to himself as he walks toward me, but as soon as he looks at me, his eyes light up. "Bianca," he says like he knows exactly who I am. "Vinnie's told me a lot about you."

More heat creeps up my neck, filling my cheeks, which I didn't think was possible because I'm already completely embarrassed by the greeting his family is giving me.

"He has?" I turn and eye Vinnie, wondering what he's been saying about me.

Vinnie pulls me back to his side. "Was I right, Pop?"

"You were right, son. Beautiful and smart. I'm Santino," he tells me as he grabs my hand and brings it to his lips. "But you can call me Tino." He sweeps his lips across the top of my hand ever so lightly.

The men in this family have charm, looks, and more muscles than human beings should be allowed to have. It's ridiculous. It's like I stepped into one of my books. But it's not fantasy; it's reality.

"Tino," Vinnie's mother says, pushing him away from me. "Stop pawing the poor girl." She hooks her arm through mine and ushers me toward the kitchen with Vinnie still attached to me. "We're eating in ten."

I fully expect the rest of the family to go back to what they were doing before we arrived, but they don't. They follow us and take seats around the large table as Vinnie pulls out a chair for me.

To say this is overwhelming is an understatement. "You should've warned me," I say as he kisses my cheek, but I keep my voice low enough so no one else can hear over their own chatter.

"So, Bianca, what do you write?" Daphne holds a bottle of wine in the air, tipping it toward me.

I nod because even though it's barely noon, I could use a drink. "I write novels."

"Romance novels," Vinnie adds. "Hot as hell ones, too."

Daphne's face lights up, and she glances at Tilly and Delilah. "We love a hot read. Maybe we've read you. What's your writing name?"

"Bianca May."

"Oh. My. God. No way."

"Way," I say with a smile, assuming she's read a book or at least heard of me somewhere.

"We have two celebrities sitting at the table," Tilly says with a small chuckle. "A superstar quarterback and a big-time romance author."

"I don't know about all that."

"Don't be modest, sweetheart," Tilly says. "Take credit where credit is due."

"I love your books," Daphne says, "and I agree with Tilly. You're a rock star."

Mrs. Gallo comes to stand at the edge of the table, again wielding the spatula she had in her hand when we first arrived. "Should I read them?"

"No. Don't." My answer is quick and confident. The last thing I want is my guy's mom reading my books.

My guy?

Oh sweet Jesus.

Now I'm starting to sound like Vinnie. Where did that come from? I'm still in my don't-have-time-for-a-man-or-the-distraction hiatus, or at least, that's what I keep telling myself.

In the last ten days, I've spent more time with Vinnie than I did with some of my past boyfriends I'd dated for months.

"Ma, they're right up your alley," Delilah tells her as I fidget with my hands in my lap, trying to stop myself from running out of here in sheer panic.

"How dirty?" Mrs. Gallo asks.

"Dirty with a capital D." Daphne laughs.

"Must be great to date a romance writer." Lucio smirks.

Vinnie rubs the back of his neck because he's seen the reality that is an author's life. Romance or not, I'm a hot mess, locked away in my apartment and sometimes not smelling or looking my best.

"It's different." He slides his arm under the table and places his hand on top of mine.

"Maybe she can teach you about romance," Angelo says as he crosses his arms, giving Vinnie a funny look.

I grab my wineglass with my free hand, gulping it down like I've been walking in the desert for days.

"I know all about romance, brother."

"Fine." Angelo sighs. "Maybe she can teach you about love."

I choke and start coughing uncontrollably. Vinnie rubs my back, and the entire table goes silent. Although I'm gasping for air, at least no one's talking about love, romance, or being a couple anymore.

"Are you okay, baby?" Vinnie asks with those big green eyes, looking so damn cute.

I nod and clear my throat, trying to wipe away the tears from my eyes. "I'm great. Never better," I rasp.

"How's training camp going?" Mr. Gallo asks like he's reading my mind and throwing a Hail Mary my way.

"It's great." Vinnie's hand hasn't left my body. "I think I have it locked down."

"Is the position the only thing you locked down?"

Angelo shifts his eyes to me and then back to his brother.

Vinnie leans forward, eyes narrowed on Angelo. "I'll have it all locked down soon."

"What are we talking about?" Tilly asks as the cutest little girl I've ever seen climbs into her lap.

"Nothing," Angelo says, smiling at his girl.

"Whatcha want, baby doll?" Tilly asks the little girl.

"That's Angelo's kid, Tate," Vinnie whispers in my ear.

"I was wondering…" Tate pauses like the wheels are spinning in her head or she knows what she's about to ask is something big enough that she needs to draw it out as long as possible. "If maybe after dinner…" She toys with the necklace around Tilly's neck and looks at her with the biggest puppy-dog eyes I've ever seen. "… I can pick out two cupcakes for dessert."

"Just one, Tate," Angelo tells her.

Tate's shoulders sag forward. "Please," she begs Tilly like she didn't even hear her father.

Tilly brushes a few strands of hair behind Tate's ear. "Your daddy said one."

Tate lets out a loud huff. "Fine, but I'm picking out the biggest one I can find."

Tilly laughs. "Whatever you want, sugar."

"Everyone, off their ass. The food's ready," Mrs. Gallo says with her back to us as she opens the oven door.

Vinnie leans over. "Her cooking sucks. Just be warned. Don't take too much."

I lift my eyebrows, figuring with all these kids, she was probably an excellent cook. None of them look like they've missed a meal a day in their entire life.

"Okay," I whisper with my mouth so close to his, I could kiss him.

That's the problem.

I haven't wanted a man as badly as I want him in so long. That should be a great thing for someone who lives romance. But for a girl on a deadline, it's the worst possible thing ever.

Instead of pecking away at the keyboard, I'm daydreaming about Vinnie and his big hands, not to mention the other parts of him that set my body on fire.

How in the hell did I let myself fall for a guy this hard and this fast when I've sworn off men?

It's the Vinnie Gallo effect, and I am swept up in it.

CHAPTER 16
VINNIE

I HAVEN'T SEEN Bianca in five days. Training camp has been grueling, and by the time I get home, I'm completely wiped out. My arm is sore, along with everything else in my body, and I spend hours icing my shoulder while sitting on my couch dozing off or reading that dirty book I snagged from her coffee table.

College Vinnie is gone. The days of partying and then getting by on my God-given talent aren't enough anymore. Everything is bigger. We run harder, pushing our bodies to the max even when doing more doesn't seem possible.

Bianca and I have texted off and on, but she says she's busy working and that I'm a distraction. I know she's on a deadline, but the girl has to come up for air sometime. She needs to eat, take care of herself, and step away from the keyboard every once in a while, or she's going to wear herself out.

I'm standing outside her door with a complete

arsenal of things to help her relax. Chinese food and pizza, wine, a candle that's supposed to help with concentration, and me. It's Friday night and I have two days off to recuperate, and nothing sounds better than a little Bianca time. After I hounded her for hours, she finally relented and said she'd take a break from her words tonight.

She opens the door, and my heart skips. Bianca's wearing those yoga pants I love so much, the ones that show every curve and swell of her ass. The small tank top doesn't leave anything to the imagination either, and the fact that she isn't wearing a bra makes it damn near impossible for me to keep my eyes off her breasts.

"Hey," she says while I stand there gawking at her like I've never seen a woman before. "Come in."

She tries to take the bag and pizza box from my hand, but I shake my head. "I got this. You just relax tonight. I don't want you lifting a finger."

Her body moves backward as I walk into her place, wearing less clothing than she is. It's part of my plan. She keeps giving me the runaround, talking about her break from men and sex, but so far, I'm two-for-two on orgasms and her breaking that promise she keeps throwing around like a security blanket.

She follows me to the couch and stands next to me as I unpack the bag of food. I glance up, catching her checking out my biceps, licking those beautiful lips like she's ready to eat me instead of the takeout.

"Hungry?"

She nods, finally noticing that I'm watching her as she stares at me. "I haven't eaten all day."

"Baby." I grab her hand, pulling her down to the floor in front of the coffee table with me. "You have to take better care of yourself. That mind of yours needs fuel to create, and so does your body. No more skipping meals. Coffee is not a food group."

She scrunches up her face. "It keeps me going."

I grab her hands, holding them tight. "Do I need to have food delivered to you to make sure you're taking care of yourself while I'm working?"

She stares at me, not speaking, just blinking like I'm saying something she doesn't quite understand.

"Better yet, I'll have my chef prep your meals for the week, so I don't have to worry."

"I do fine, Vinnie. Don't be silly." She lets out a little huff. "You have a chef?"

"I'm on a strict diet during camp." I run my hand down my chest, taunting her a little because she keeps staring at me like I'm dinner. "Got to keep this body in top shape for the long season ahead."

Her eyes follow my hand and linger. "It looks pretty good to me," she says softly.

"You want to touch it, don't you?" I smirk.

"You're so full of yourself." She smacks my shoulder, but I know the truth. "I'm starving."

"Lucky for you, tonight's my cheat night, or else we'd be having chicken and broccoli."

She frowns. "That doesn't sound so awful."

I unpack the bag, taking out the five small

containers of food I ordered. "It is compared to this. I got a little of everything because I wasn't sure what you liked."

"I'm easy."

I watch her as she opens the containers, and I know she's the opposite of easy. If she were, I already would've slept with her. But Bianca isn't like most women I've known. Maybe that's what I like most about her. She's real and doesn't give two shits about who I am, what I do, or how much money I have in the bank.

"Want to watch *Scandalous Reign*?"

Her beautiful, full lips turn up. "I haven't had time all week. Are you sure?"

"I told you I love that show." I grab the remote and hand it to her. "Put it on."

As soon as the episode starts, I know I've hit the jackpot. I remember exactly what happens when Princess Viktoria is being courted. This is hands down the sexiest episode of the entire series.

"I can't imagine being betrothed to someone you've never met," Bianca says before shoving a forkful of lo mein into her mouth.

"That's because you believe in love, but their marriage is only about power and the bloodline."

Her eyes are glued to the television. "She's in love with Richard, though. My heart's going to break into a million little pieces."

Richard is an earl and doesn't have a high enough title or the royal blood to get the girl he wants. Viktoria's a princess and the oldest child of the king and queen and totally screwed at this point. Richard and Viktoria have kissed throughout the show, always fading to black to leave the audience wondering exactly what happened, but in this episode, before she says her wedding vows…they show everything.

"Oh my God," Bianca whispers. "Are they going to do it?" She glances at me with wide eyes before turning back to the screen before I can answer.

They very much do *it*, and it's hot as fuck too. Bianca's fork is in front of her mouth, but she isn't eating. She can't take her eyes off the television as Richard's fingers work the ties on the back of Viktoria's dress. When it slips to the floor, exposing her backside to the camera, Bianca sucks in a breath and rocks backward.

The dress is pooled at Viktoria's feet as Richard squeezes her ass, and he kisses her deeply. It's soft-core porn, but there's something about the fact that their love and this act are forbidden that makes it even hotter.

Bianca squirms so slightly, I almost don't notice. "I've been waiting forever for this," she says.

"It's worth the wait. Trust me."

"Everything that's good usually is."

I smile, staring at her profile and picking at my pizza, finding food not all that interesting when compared to Bianca. She's oblivious to the fact that I'm watching her and not the television as I rake my eyes over her body, soaking in all her hotness.

She's naturally beautiful. Even when she's wearing

barely any makeup, I'd call her drop-dead gorgeous. Most women I've been with typically look nothing like the person I went to bed with when I wake up the next morning. It was like waking up with a complete stranger instead of the girl I was balls deep in the night before. But that's not Bianca. Everything about her is real.

She places her fork down on the table and covers her face with her hands. "Oh God, they're going to get caught. I can't look."

"They don't get caught."

She turns her face, opening her fingers to see me. "Do not ruin this for me."

"Ruin what? Your eyes are covered. You're not even watching."

She lifts her chin as her hand falls away from her eyes. "I am watching. Do not tell me what's going to happen."

"Then watch. It's about to get good."

She grunts as she turns back toward the television. "You're probably the same asshole who reads the last chapter of a book before starting the first page."

"I am not."

She waves me off and shushes me like my talking is making it impossible for her to follow what's going on, even though they're not speaking. The only sounds in the apartment are the moans coming from the television. Bianca's breathing slows as she stares at the screen, and Richard takes the princess's nipple in his mouth as he lays her on the bed and slides between her legs. The angle changes to a view from above, showing the guy's entire ass, which isn't even that impressive, but Bianca shifts backward as Richard rocks into Viktoria over and over again until finally fading to black.

I scoot closer to Bianca and touch her hand. She glances at me, and at first, I think she's going to tell me off again. But instead, she darts her tongue out and sweeps it across her lips. My cock twitches, growing harder and throbbing for some relief.

"Let me see you naked," she says so innocently, like she's asking what the weather's like outside.

"What?" I'm pretty sure I didn't hear her right and that my cock has somehow taken over my brain.

"Take off your clothes. I want to look at you."

"Now?"

She nods, and that damn tongue comes back out, sweeping across those full lips again. "Yes, now."

Never the type to be bashful, I stand quickly and pull down my pants. When my cock springs free and waves as I straighten my body, her eyes widen. Her face is only a few feet from my cock, her eyes staring at my dick like she's never seen anything more amazing.

She moves closer, eyes locked on my cock. "Touch it," she tells me. "Put your hand around it, and stroke yourself."

I didn't come here to jack myself off, but if this is what it takes to make Bianca happy, I'll do it.

She parts her lips as I palm my cock and wrap my fingers around the shaft. "Your body's perfect," she says, sweeping her eyes up my abs before sliding them right back to my dick. "It's like a work of art. You're so hard...everywhere."

"This is because of you, Bianca." I stroke harder, gripping my cock so tightly, my hips move to chase my palm.

In all my sexual experiences, I don't think I've ever rubbed one out in front of a chick. That I could do alone, and I've never found the thought all that appealing. But with the way she's looking at me, telling me how to touch myself, it's the biggest turn-on in the world.

She reaches out and touches my legs, gripping my thighs with both her hands as she scoots across the floor. She's so close, I can feel her warm breath brushing against the head of my cock, only making me harder.

She turns my body and rests her back against the couch, facing the television and my cock. The moaning returns from Viktoria and Richard going at it again, and one of Bianca's hands leaves my leg. My eyes follow its movement, and I nearly swallow my tongue as she dips her fingers into the waistband of her yoga pants.

There I am, standing completely naked, stroking my cock, while this hot-as-fuck girl touches herself and watches me.

This woman has me all kinds of sideways.

I'm pretty sure this is the best Friday night I've ever had, and I know in an instant there's no place I'd rather be.

CHAPTER 17
BIANCA

VINNIE PLACES two fingers under my chin, tipping my head back. "This isn't right," he says softly, still stroking his cock with one hand. "I need to be inside you."

His eyes move to my hand, which is still inside my yoga pants, working my clit. I'm so close to orgasm. So close, my damn toes are curling, and the last thing I want to do is stop.

"I want to kiss your beautiful lips as you moan my name and come with my cock buried so deep inside you, you'll feel me there long after I've left."

He says such dirty and delicious things. Just like the guys I write in my books. And just like them too, his body is pure perfection. I could watch him touch himself all night and never grow bored.

There's something so sexy about the way a man touches himself. It's always been a secret obsession I've had, and my internet browsing history is proof.

I want to have sex with him. What woman in her right mind wouldn't? But we've already muddied the waters so quickly, I'm not ready for the next step. I know Vinnie's type. Notorious playboy who jumps from woman to woman like it's an Olympic sport. Sure, he wants me, but he's all about the chase.

The moment I give in and surrender myself to him completely, he'll hop to the next because he'll have taken what he wanted.

I move my head away from his fingers and scoot forward as he continues to stroke his cock with his other hand. Even with him saying all the right things, I know having sex with him at this moment would be all kinds of bad for my head. I line my mouth up with his cock and peer up at him with a small grin. I stick out my tongue, swiping it across the soft head of his dick.

He rocks backward as he sucks in a harsh breath. "You don't play fair."

I reach behind him, placing my hand on his ass, which is rock-hard and fucking spectacular. "I need to taste you." I smirk, knowing I have him right where I want him.

He doesn't argue. What man would? I pull him toward me, opening my mouth and closing my lips around the head of his cock. He moans as his hand falls away from his shaft, and he thrusts forward, giving me exactly what I want.

His body shakes with pleasure as I take him deeper, sliding his hard, velvety length against my tongue until my gag reflex starts to kick in. Although I want my orgasm almost as much as I need air in my lungs, I have to control the depth of his cock and give him an orgasm that's going to rock his world.

"Oh God. Just like that," he says as I wrap my hand around his slick shaft. He tangles his fingers in my hair, tightening his hold as I grip him roughly and suck him off like a pro.

There's something so powerful about giving head. Holding a man in my hands and loving him with my mouth until he's spiraling to orgasm so quickly, his knees practically give out.

I work his length, twisting my hand and creating a perfect connection with my lips. I go all out, giving him everything I've got until my eyes water and my jaw aches. I look up as he stiffens and his eyes close, lips parted and looking hotter than ever. When his body starts to shake uncontrollably, I know I have him.

I use my hand more, leaving my tongue on the top of the head and working the sensitive spot underneath. The last thing I want to do is have him squirt down my throat, making me gag and heave because, let's face it… come isn't the tasty life-force I claim it is in my romance novels.

Vinnie doesn't seem to notice as his body rocks backward and forward, fucking my wet hand and my soft lips. He calls out my name as I pull my mouth away, watching his body ride the waves of orgasm. I slow my pace, drawing every aftershock out of him before finally releasing my hold on him.

He opens his eyes and peers down at me. He sees

his come dripping from my hand and not neatly deposited in my mouth like a porn star who deep-throats for a living. "That was…"

He doesn't finish the statement. He doesn't have to for me to know I rocked his world. The way his body moved and he gasped for air, I know the orgasm tore through him like a hurricane.

There's a knock on the door, and I jump to my feet like the Karate Kid. I take in a very naked Vinnie with his cock that still looks ready for action, which should be impossible.

"Put your pants on," I tell him as I grab the napkins off the coffee table and wipe my hands.

There's a second knock. "Bianca, come on. Open up. I know you're home," Luis says, always having the worst timing.

I don't have to look in the mirror to know I look like a deer in headlights. "Fuck," I hiss and push Vinnie toward the bedroom as soon as he scoops his pants off the floor. "He can't see you here."

Vinnie looks at me over his shoulder, laughing because I'm panicked and almost insane. "Why?"

"He'll kill you." I push harder against his back, but he's like moving a brick wall.

"You overreact, baby."

"Bianca," Luis says louder. "I can see the lights on in your place." That goddamn little slit under the door will be the death of me—or Vinnie, if Luis finds him here.

"Coming!" I yell.

"Yes, yes, I did." Vinnie laughs.

I smack his ass as he finally steps foot in my bedroom. "Do not come out. Do you understand?"

"So, what do I do?" He looks around my super girlie bedroom that looks like a unicorn threw up all over it.

"Just relax. Lie down. Take a nap. I don't care. Just don't come out."

Vinnie laughs as he sits down on the edge of my bed, naked and holding his pants. "I'm sure I can keep myself busy in here."

I don't have time to think about all the sexy things in my drawers or the fact that the hot-ass pro baller is in my bedroom, naked and waiting. I close the bedroom door and run through the living room, stubbing my toe on the coffee table.

I screech in pain and grab my foot, bouncing on the other foot as I make it to the door. "This better be good," I say as I open the door to Luis and a woman I've never seen before.

"Hey, sis." Luis smiles. "This is Karen."

Karen looks like every other floozy he's ever been with. Teased hair, tits hanging out, red lipstick, and nothing but trouble. That's my brother's type. It's entirely okay for him to whore himself around, but God forbid, I actually want to be with a man, and my brother completely overreacts.

"Hey, Karen." I plaster on a fake smile and somehow resist the urge to punch Luis in the face.

Karen giggles and pops her gum. "Hi. I'm such a huge fan."

The urge to roll my eyes is almost overwhelming, but I hold my shit together. "Oh. Thank you so much. That's really kind of you."

I'm thankful for every reader and fan, but right now, the last thing I want to do is chitchat about my writing with my brother's flavor of the night while Vinnie's come dries between my fingers.

Luis walks by me with Karen under his arm and enters my apartment without an invitation. "Do you have company?" he asks, turning to face me.

I shake my head. "I was just really hungry. It's my Netflix and chill night."

Luis's eyebrows draw downward. "Your what?"

"I order food and binge television."

"Bianca, you're too young to sit at home and watch television on a Friday night. Live a little already."

I cross my arms over my chest and cock my head. "I am living. I like my life. Are you here to shit on it, or did you come here for a reason?"

"I wanted to invite you out with us tonight. We're going to the new club down the street. Figured I'd stop in and ask if you'd like to join us."

"Sweetheart," Karen says, sliding her arm around his middle. "I have to use the little girls' room."

Luis ticks his head backward. "Down the hall," he says to her. She giggles as Luis pinches her ass. "Go ahead, doll."

I glare at my brother as Karen heads toward the bathroom. "I can't believe you just dropped by like this with some girl."

"She's not *some* girl. She's Karen." Luis runs his fingers through his dark, floppy hair. "Isn't she great?"

"Oh yeah. She's perfect," I say sarcastically.

Karen screams and Luis turns. My eyes follow the noise, seeing Karen standing in the doorway to my bedroom with her eyes practically coming out of her head like an old cartoon.

"Who are you?" she asks.

"Hey," Vinnie says, and I know shit's about to go down.

I glance at my brother, who's staring at me so hard, I'm shocked death rays aren't flying out of his eye sockets. "Company?"

"Just a friend."

"Is it that guy you brought to the party?" The vein running down the middle of Luis's forehead is big and angry, as if it's about to burst at any moment.

"Guy?" I laugh. "It's none of your business." I look over my brother's shoulder, finding Karen hasn't moved. She's just gawking at a hopefully only half-naked Vinnie. "Next door, Karen."

My brother starts toward my bedroom, but I use my body as a human shield. "You better move," he tells me, like somehow, he's become my protector and my father.

"This is my house, Luis." I hold out my arms, leaving him no way to get around me as we stand at the entrance to the hallway.

"You better get your ass out here, you punk," Luis calls out, practically foaming at the mouth.

"You stay in there!" I yell over my shoulder because

the last thing I need is Vinnie and Luis getting into a fight. "You need to take *Karen* and leave."

Luis's dark eyes narrow. "He's not right for you. He's using you, Bianca."

I laugh bitterly. "Maybe I'm using him, brother. Ever think of that?"

Luis straightens, but his glare is still icy cold. "You trust too easy."

"I trust no one," I tell him. The reality of my words hits me. I don't trust anyone anymore. Not after the way men have treated me in the past.

Karen comes bouncing out of the bathroom like she's oblivious to the shitstorm she's created. "Nice to meet you," she says to Vinnie as she passes by the bedroom.

"You too," he replies, and a small piece of me dies.

Luis and I are staring each other down as Karen wraps an arm around his back. "I'm ready, Daddy."

I almost puke at the nickname. There's something so wrong with women who call men "Daddy." In role-playing or BDSM, I can tolerate it, but in real life, standing in front of his family, it's totally disgusting.

"Yeah, Daddy, you better go."

Luis snakes his arm around Karen's shoulders, but he hasn't looked at her yet. He's too busy giving me the death stare to look down. "He and I are going to have words."

"You want to have them now?" Vinnie says from behind me.

My brother's hard stare slices to my bedroom, and I

know I've got to defuse the situation, or you know, remind Luis who's boss.

"Get out." I point toward the doorway, blocking my brother's ability to get down the hall and try to beat the piss out of Vinnie. I turn toward Vinnie. "Go back into my bedroom and shut up."

Vinnie's eyebrows rise before a smile creeps across his lips. "Yes, ma'am. I like it when you're bossy."

I glare toward the ceiling and mutter a string of curse words. "Go, Luis, and take Karen with you."

"We're still going to have words."

I roll my eyes. "Not tonight, big brother."

"Leave your sister alone, Daddy. She's living life. She's young. Let her have fun. Would you rather she be all alone here tonight?"

Luis's hard glare softens, but he doesn't relax. "No." He sighs. "But I still don't like it."

"You're not supposed to. She's your sister, but damn, man, give her some space. She's got a hottie in her bedroom. That sounds like a solid Friday night. Do you want to have fun with me, Daddy, or stay here and argue?"

I want to puke. There's something about Karen and Luis that activates my gag reflex worse than deep-throating a cock. I cover my mouth and swallow, somehow keeping down the Chinese food.

"You're right, beautiful. Let's get out of here. My sister and I will talk another day."

"Oh, goodie. I can hardly wait," I say behind the hand that's still covering my mouth.

Luis stares at me for a few more seconds. "Be smart, Bianca."

"Sure thing, Daddy." I nod.

He grumbles but finally moves as Karen pulls him toward the door. "Don't worry. We'll have more fun without her. Remember when I..." She leans over, whispering something in his ear.

Whatever she says has Luis out the door and gone without another word. After the door slams, Vinnie doesn't come out, and there's not a single sound coming from my bedroom.

"Vinnie, you can come out."

"Come here," he calls out. "I want to show you something."

I'm sure he does, and it's probably about nine inches and hard as a rock.

As I step into the doorway, I see Vinnie still very naked and holding a pair of nipple clamps that were in my nightstand drawer. "What are these?"

"They're nipple clamps." I shrug.

"I know that. I mean, do you use them?" He stares at the shiny metal, his cock bobbing and waving at the very thought of those hugging my nipples.

"Yes."

"Alone?"

"Yes." I'm not ashamed. I use every toy I write about in my books. How can I describe the sensation something delivers without testing it out on myself first?

"Ever use them with anybody?"

I shake my head.

He motions for me to come to him, but I don't move. "Come on, baby. Lemme rock your world."

"We're not fucking," I tell him. I'm not ready to take that step with him. Not yet.

A wicked smile plays on his lips. "Who said anything about that?" He dangles the nipple clamps from his fingers. "I have an orgasm or two to repay and a drawer full of toys to make it happen."

Fuck. This man's going to be the death of me.

CHAPTER 18
VINNIE

"HOW DID you know Tilly was the one?"

Angelo studies me as he leans against the bar with a toothpick between his lips. "This girl got you questioning your ways?"

The last few days, I've been doing nothing but thinking about Bianca. I've never been this way with any girl in my entire life, especially not one I haven't slept with.

"I don't have any ways."

Angelo stares at me and raises an eyebrow.

"Okay. Okay." I throw up my hands because my brother knows everything there is to know about me. "I like this chick."

There's a hint of a smile on Angelo's face. "When was the last time you were with someone else?"

I open my mouth to throw out a date and quickly close it again. I was all ready to fire off an answer, but this is something I really have to think about. "It's been a while." I rub the back of my neck and stare down at the bar top. "Shit, it's been a few months. I've been so busy with training camp, I didn't have time to get laid."

"But now you have time?"

I shake my head. "Not really, but I make time for Bianca."

He pulls the toothpick from his lips and smirks. "I think you answered your own question."

I stare at him for a minute with my mouth hanging open, letting his words sink in before I finally speak. "Just because I drop by her place doesn't mean I'm ready to spend the rest of my life with her."

He shakes his head slowly and sighs. "Have you ever *made* time for the other women?"

The truth of my words puts shit into perspective. I *make* time for her. I go out of my way to see her on the weekends, even though she isn't exactly overly thrilled when I don't give her an option.

"Well." I pause and swallow down the reality that my brother may, in fact, be right. I was more of an in-the-moment type of guy, and I had never been into seconds either. "No."

He rests his elbows against the bar and leans forward. "You want her dating other men?"

"Fuck no." I look at him like he's insane because he should know me better than that.

"Point made." He smiles.

I walked right into that one. I never once cared about what happened to the women I slept with after the fact.

Hell, I didn't even care if they left my bed and gave someone else sloppy seconds. But the very thought of any man touching Bianca sets my blood on fire.

"I would break his legs."

"Did you lock it down?"

I stare at him, and he stares back.

He motions between us. "I remember you being all up in my shit about locking down Tilly, and the same when Lucio was dating Delilah."

"Yeah, well. You guys are different," I grumble.

Angelo has always been a relationship kind of guy. He started dating Marissa so long ago, I don't remember a time in my childhood without her. And although it took him a while to move on after her death, he went right into another lasting relationship.

Lucio is a different beast. He was a mix of Angelo and me. He had been a playboy at his core, but he had way more feelings for the women he slept with than I ever did. His getting caught up on Delilah and Lulu wasn't surprising, especially with his hero syndrome.

"Grow the fuck up," Angelo says and points at me. "You either lock it down or move the fuck on. Shit or get off the pot, brother. Stop stringing her along."

I rock back on my stool. "It's the other way around. Bianca keeps pushing me away." I shrug because I can't figure the girl out. "One minute, we're bumping and grinding our way to ecstasy. And the next, she's pushing me out the door."

"Ahh." He laughs. "Getting a taste of your own

medicine." I give him the middle finger, which only makes him laugh harder. "You know what they say?"

"No." I cross my arms, suddenly defensive, and purse my lips. "I don't believe in any of that nonsense."

"The girls usually throw themselves at you."

"Older women too." I wink.

Angelo rolls his eyes. "The first girl to turn her back on you has your head all messed up."

"She's not turning her back on me."

He tilts his head. "She's not?"

"Not exactly."

"Have you slept with her?"

I focus on my fingertips as I tap them against the wooden bar and avoid looking at Angelo. "That's kind of personal, isn't it?"

His laugh echoes in the empty bar. "That's precious coming from you."

"Fine. We haven't had sex," I blurt out. "Happy?"

"The fact that you're sticking around this long without sleeping with her shows you're growing up and may actually want more out of the relationship than a quick lay."

"Ang." I lean back and bring my eyes to his. "I've never been a quick lay."

He grunts before throwing a rag from the countertop in my face. "You still act like a dumbass. That much hasn't changed."

I crumple the damp cloth in my hand. "Seriously, though. I can't mess this up. We're neighbors, and I'll still have to see her every day if I do."

"So, you haven't slept with her because you're a pussy?"

I groan. "Of course, fucker. Bianca's different."

He steps backward and leans against the countertop behind him. "You're a pussy." He crosses his arms with a satisfied smile on his face. "This girl is into romance. She doesn't want the playboy Vinnie Gallo. She wants to know she isn't going to land in a tabloid as the latest side piece of the hottest player in Chicago, and I'm not talking about football."

"So, some sort of grand gesture?"

My brain hurts from thinking this hard. I've never had to think beyond a smile and a wink before the chick's clothes would practically fall off and she'd be on her knees sucking me off.

"A sincere gesture. It doesn't need to be big, but it has to have meaning." Angelo glances toward the door. "Go let Carlos in. He's getting antsy out there and probably scaring the pedestrians."

"I'm going to jet. I have to get to the training facility. If I'm late, the coach will have my balls," I tell him as I walk toward the doorway where Carlos has his face practically smashed against the glass.

"He'll have to wait in line behind Bianca."

I flip him off, hearing his laughter at the hilarity of my predicament and all the snarky comments he's able to hurl my way.

"Hey, kid." Carlos smiles, and the lines in his face deepen as I open the door for him. "You look a mess."

"I've never been better. Training camp's brutal," I lie.

I am a mess. I'm used to working my ass off on the field, but working Bianca is the hardest thing I've had to do in years. They say nothing worth having in life comes easy, but it shouldn't be this goddamn hard either.

"Go make us proud," he says as he walks by me, needing his morning beer to straighten his drunk old ass out.

I spend the next thirty minutes while driving to training camp trying to think of all the grand gestures I could make to win over Bianca. Most of them involve money, but I'm not sure something splashy and over the top like whisking her away to Vegas for a weekend would be something a writer on a deadline would like.

Her career is just as important as mine. I live game to game, and she lives book to book. We are only as good as our next play. The last thing I want is for her to get distracted from finishing her book and missing her deadline. That would kill any future chance of making her my girl faster than treating her like a quick lay.

I'm not even paying attention to where I'm walking as I make my way down the hallway to the locker room.

"Hey, handsome." The voice crawls over my skin, making me suddenly feel ill. "I've been waiting for you."

I sidestep Tracie as she tries to touch me. "You're not allowed to be here."

She pouts, but it has zero effect on me. "Don't be that way. You know we're meant to be together."

"I have a girlfriend," I tell her, tucking my hands into my pockets as I put more space between us.

"We all slum it sometimes," she says with a shrug.

Her words slam into me, and I see red. I stalk toward her, getting in her face, but I am careful not to touch her. "Let's get something straight...again. I am not yours. You're not mine. We're not a couple. Bianca's my girl, you crazy bitch."

The insane part of her takes over, and she laughs right in my face. "You're precious with how much you defend your little toy. Have your fun now, Vinnie. Sow your oats. It doesn't matter to me. I know who you're going to be with in the end."

I narrow my eyes, trying to calm down because my body's vibrating with anger. "We are nothing."

"Gallo," Coach calls from the door of his office down the hallway, probably saving me from doing or saying something I'll regret.

"This is the last time I'm going to tell you to leave me alone." I don't give her another chance to say something back before I jog toward the coach's office, trying to shake off the tightness in my body from Tracie's bullshit.

"What's up, Coach?" I say when I am face-to-face with him.

He's standing in the doorway, arms crossed, his eyes going between Tracie and me. "Step inside," he tells me. "We need to talk."

I pace the small empty patch of linoleum in front of his desk, waiting for him to speak. He walks through his office slowly before collapsing into his chair. "Stop moving. You're making me nervous, for shit's sake."

I stop quickly and turn to face him. "What's being done about her?"

He lets out a heavy sigh before shuffling papers around his extremely messy desk. "She's seeing her psychiatrist again and back on the meds, but her grandfather can't bar her from the facility, though she's no longer allowed in the locker room."

"That's it?" I glance up toward the ceiling and curse under my breath.

"If she becomes more aggressive, her parents are willing to get her treatment in a facility, but right now, this is the best we can do."

"So, all that shit about me being the future of the team?" I ball my hands into tight fists at my sides and bite down my anger. The last thing I want is to give anyone a reason to cut me from the team before the season even starts.

"It's still true. Listen, you have a few options."

I cross my arms over my chest and lift my chin. I'm pretty sure they're all going to suck, but I don't tell Coach that.

"One, you just hang tight and wait for her to find a new infatuation."

"Victim," I mumble because infatuations can be something great, but not when Tracie's involved.

"Coach, she's been after me for almost a year. I don't see her moving on any time soon."

"Two," he says, skipping right over what I just said. "You can file a TRO against her, but the likelihood it'll be put in place and followed is highly doubtful. Plus, it'll end up in the hands of the press. No longer will the story be about the superstar kid who's going to take his hometown team to the play-offs. It'll be about your relationship with the owner's granddaughter."

"There's no relationship," I correct him.

"Or we sit back and wait for her to really fuck up."

"That's all you have?" I shake my head slowly and groan.

"That's it, kid."

I don't say another word before I storm out of his office, finding the hallway empty, and head toward the locker room. In a few short months, my life has gone from uncomplicated to crazy-as-fuck without any middle ground.

CHAPTER 19
BIANCA

"NOW THAT WE have the niceties out of the way," my agent says as she pushes aside her empty plate. "I wanted to talk to you about your current project." Her face is tight, and nothing about her smile is sincere.

"Okay," I say the words, drawing them out because if Susan has dropped everything to fly to Chicago to meet with me, the news probably isn't good.

I've been with Susan Williams, one of the biggest romance agents in the world, for almost four years. She took a chance on me when no one else would. Others claimed I was too young or too inexperienced to have a successful writing career, but not Susan.

Most of the time, I'm grateful to have her in my life.

Then there're times like this, when she's about to school me in the ways of publishing, where I want to cover my ears and run out of the room before she makes me feel as small as an ant.

Susan leans over, digging into her oversized purse

and pulling out a giant stack of papers. "I had a lengthy conversation with your editor after you sent us the first half."

I pull my hands back into my lap, balling them into tight fists. I'm prepping for a mental and verbal ass-beating with no recourse but to sit here and take it.

"Okay," I repeat as my lunch churns in my stomach.

She removes the giant clip holding the sheets together and flips the title page over, exposing the first page of my upcoming book. All I see is red. Not from anger, but from the critical ink of my editor's pen.

"I'm just going to be honest and get to the point quickly."

I don't know if she thinks those words are going to bring me solace, but they don't. My heart's pounding and my hands are sweating as I dig my fingernails into the fleshy part of my palms.

"The beginning of the story isn't what your readers typically expect. It's a super slow start and does not capture anyone's attention. The entire first few chapters need to be reworked."

"I thought it was sweet." The smile I give her is pained.

She waves her hand over the stack of papers and shakes her head. "Sweetie, your readers don't want sweet. They want hot and fast."

"The story is hot," I argue and sit up a little straighter than I had been a moment ago.

I've pulled out all the stops on this one, giving my readers everything I know they love. The hero is a hot alpha with a mouth on him that'll make any woman's heart skip a few beats.

"The beginning needs more punch, and a sex scene or two would be nice too. What's going on in your life? Sometimes, our real world causes issues in our fictional one."

"Nothing's changed," I lie.

She raises one overly plucked eyebrow. "Still going through your man hiatus?"

I nod slowly. "Sort of."

"Oh?" Now, both of her eyebrows are up. "What's 'sort of' mean, exactly?"

"A few weeks ago, I started seeing someone."

"That explains it, then," she says, running her hand up and down the top sheet of paper. "The chapters you've sent me recently have become more intense and steamier. You can clearly tell when you were without a man. It shows in your work."

"I don't agree."

"Read over the first few chapters. You'll see there's a huge difference—and not a good one either."

Susan's trying to be nice, I know she is, but her words still sting. They always do. In the end, and I'll never admit this to her, she's almost always right. She's never been one to blow smoke up my ass and tell me something is great. And because of her inability to lie, I always publish a better book.

"Whatever's going on in your personal life has major effects on your writing. I know why you swore off men for a little while, sweetie, but when you're writing spicy romance...men are part of the business. You can't be sour on love and try to pull emotion from your readers."

"Fine," I snap. "I'll rework the beginning, but I'll need a few more weeks."

"We can give you two more weeks to get the final draft on my desk."

I rock backward. "Two weeks? It took me a month to write those first few chapters."

She pushes the manuscript across the table. "You better find some inspiration in the arms of that man of yours and get typing."

I'm almost in tears by the time I hail a cab and climb into the back seat. I flip through the manuscript, ignoring the traffic and the super chatty cab driver, as I read through the comments left by my agent and editor.

Every book is a small piece of my soul, and their red slashes and critical words cut me deeply. No one wants to hear how dreadful something they've created is. Nothing kills enthusiasm for a writer more than being told something flat out sucks.

I'm so in my head, tears streaming down my face and clutching my manuscript to my chest, I don't even notice Vinnie standing near the elevator when I walk into the lobby.

"What's wrong?" he asks.

My eyes shift from the marble floor to his green eyes. "Just a bad day." I don't know why I lie. I don't want to be the whiny girl. The one with issues all the time. So sometimes, it's easier to pretend everything is great.

Vinnie closes the space between us, holding my arm with one hand and my face in the other. His thumb brushes against my cheek, wiping away a tear. "It looks like more than a bad day, Bianca. Tell me what happened."

"My book is shit." The tears flow harder as I say the words. The way he's looking at me doesn't help either. I sob, slurring together a string of words about how hurt I am by the comments left by my editor, but I'm pretty sure he can't understand anything I'm saying.

"Your books are great, baby." He gives me a sad smile, trying to wipe away the tears as fast as they fall.

"Not this one," I sob.

He pulls me into a tight embrace, rubbing my back and whispering soothing words. The smell and feel of Vinnie calm me, making me forget about everything Susan said. "I think we need to get out of the city for a few days," he says.

I peer up at him as I step out of his embrace. "I can't. I have to rewrite most of this damn book." I lift the manuscript I've been clutching, showing him the splotches of red everywhere.

"Bring your work with us. Maybe you'll find some inspiration."

"That's not how it works. I only write at my desk."

He raises an eyebrow. "How's that been working?"

I grumble under my breath because it's been suck-tastic according to my editor and Susan.

"Anyway, you write with a laptop. Your desk is wherever you make it."

"And what are you going to do? Just sit there and watch me work?"

He shakes his head. "I can entertain myself. Besides, I have a very strict workout regimen. I just want a few hours a day alone with you, and the rest you can work."

"I don't know. We barely know each other, Vinnie."

"Do you trust me?"

"I do."

He glances down at the manuscript as the elevator doors open. "Where does the story take place?"

"Tahiti," I say, stepping inside the tiny space with him.

"I only have four days off from camp, so that's too far, but I'll figure something out. Leave everything to me. Just pack a bag and be ready to go in the morning."

"Vinnie, I don't think we should…"

He places his finger over my lips, silencing me. "No arguments, Bianca. We both could use some time away to clear our heads."

He's right. The last thing I want to do is sit in my loft, staring out the window as the cursor blinks on the screen like it's taunting me.

"Okay."

He leans forward and cups my face in the palm of his giant hand. "Thank you," he whispers softly before pressing his lips to mine.

Suddenly, my day doesn't seem so awful. Words can be changed, and I have enough time to do it. Whatever harsh and horrible things Susan said or the editor wrote no longer seem to sting as bad.

Our kiss is broken by the familiar chime of the elevator as we arrive on our floor. "I'll text you in a little bit with the travel details. Just pack a few things—and for warm weather."

"Where are we going?"

"It's a surprise." He smiles mischievously.

Normally, surprises aren't my cup of tea, but there's something about the way he's smiling at me that has the butterflies in my stomach doing backflips. I don't remember the last time I went on vacation. It's been years since I stepped outside of my little world and remembered all the pleasure life has to offer.

CHAPTER 20
VINNIE

"THIS IS NUTS." Bianca drops her purse on the sand near the wraparound porch. "The water is so blue."

She spent the entire flight typing away furiously on her laptop, trying to work on the problems her editor and agent had told her needed to be fixed.

I studied game film and the team's playbook, hoping like hell I was ready for our first preseason game.

We each have a lot on the line. I am fighting for the starting quarterback position, and she is chasing her dreams, wanting each book to be more successful than the last.

"There's no place like the Caribbean and absolutely nothing like a private island."

The island's small but more than enough for the two of us. With no one around to bother us, we can spend a few days soaking up the sun, relaxing to the sounds of the waves lapping against the shore, and clothes are entirely optional.

Bianca stares in my direction with a smile. "You didn't have to go to all this trouble."

"You needed to get away, and to be honest, I wanted you all to myself." I lift my T-shirt over my head, exposing my chest and arms, knowing full well Bianca likes the way I look without my shirt on.

She's no longer looking at the ocean as her eyes rake over my bare chest. "We could've gone to Mackinaw or somewhere less exotic."

I grab her around the waist and haul her against my bare chest. "You can't walk around naked in Mackinaw."

I have big plans this weekend. I'm going to sweep her off her feet and make sure she knows we are meant to be together. We work. We're both workaholics, with big families, and we're just plain right together.

She swallows hard. "I can't walk around naked."

I brush the backs of my fingers against her cheek. "You wear what makes you feel comfortable, but I plan to soak up the sunshine."

"I have a swimsuit." She rests her palm against my chest and smiles up at me.

"A bikini?" I lift an eyebrow.

The thought of her in a bikini, the sun glistening off her skin dotted with water droplets has my cock hardening.

"Something like that."

I grab our bags and haul them up the stairs because

the ocean is calling my name. "Come on, babe. Let's go for a swim."

Her footsteps are heavy on the steps behind me. "I don't really love going in the ocean. Just looking at it."

I drop the bags to fish the key out of my pocket. "Just a few feet," I tell her, trying to find a happy medium.

"Sharks can get you in a foot of water."

I laugh as I put the key in the lock, opening the door. "Seriously? You think a shark is going to eat you?"

"The Bahamas have a fuckton of sharks." She grabs her suitcase from my hand and steps inside, leaving me on the patio.

"Who says?" I ask as I follow her inside.

"Google." She glances around the empty house with big eyes. "Holy shit. This place is…" Her voice trails off as her mouth hangs open.

"Ridiculous." I finish her sentence.

From the outside, it looks like a normal Caribbean home with a beautiful wraparound porch. The inside is more decadent, with oversized furniture, shiny polished-wood floors, and lush draperies.

"It's absolutely beautiful." She looks up toward the high, wood-beam ceiling. "This makes our places look boring."

I step behind her and wrap my arms around her middle. "We could get a place like this."

She glances up at me. "Getting a little ahead of yourself, aren't you?"

"We can become partners in something like this. It

would be an investment."

"I can't afford it if I don't finish this damn book."

I kiss her cheek. "Then you better go put on that bikini so we can swim, and later you can maybe get some words written."

Bianca disappears into the bedroom to change, while I open all the sliding doors and fill the place with the warm ocean breeze. I grab some beach towels and water bottles and place them on the lounge chairs on the front porch, prepping for a few hours of fun in the sun and badly needed relaxation for both of us.

The door creaks open as I walk back inside, and Bianca sticks her head out. "Close your eyes," she tells me, twisting a few pieces of her brown hair around her index finger.

I smile, feeling like a kid at Christmas before closing my eyes tightly. "Finally decide you'd rather go skinny-dipping?"

I'm crossing my fingers, hoping that's the case. The thought of her naked, the water dripping off her breasts as she comes up through a wave has my dick practically standing at attention.

"I can't go naked. Someone might see," she says, and her voice is louder, as if she's right in front of me.

"There's no one around for miles, babe," I reassure her because that's what I was promised when I booked the place.

"There are eyes everywhere."

I jostle from foot to foot because the waiting is killing me. "Can I open my eyes now?"

"Fine. You can look."

"I have to look sometime," I tell her as I slowly open my eyes. Bianca's standing in front of me with a towel wrapped around her body, and the strings of a white bathing suit peek out from underneath.

I grab the edge of the towel with two fingers. "What's with this?"

"I'm not ready for you to see my body." She bites her lips and glances down at the wood floor. "I'm embarrassed."

I take my fingers off the towel and slip them under her chin, forcing her to look at me. "Bianca, you're beautiful. Don't ever think that whatever is under that towel is going to make me feel any different."

This is classic Bianca. Most women I've been with are more than happy to get naked, showing me everything they have without hardly speaking to me first. But this girl, the one I'm falling for way too quickly, is too modest for me to see her in a swimsuit.

"I know the type of girls you date," she says with her eyes locked on mine.

I raise an eyebrow because dating is something I never do. I've never even taken another woman on a trip with me. Bianca is the first. "I think you're the most beautiful woman I've ever laid eyes on."

"I think you've been hit in the head one too many times." She smiles.

I lean forward, placing my mouth close to hers, staring into her eyes. "I like you for your bitchy attitude and strange little ways. I don't care what's underneath the towel. That's the bonus for me, baby. If it would make you more comfortable, stay in the towel, or go put on your writing outfit and swim in that."

"I can't get that wet."

I move quickly and lift her into my arms. She squeals, grabbing at the towel and holding it closed. "Either way, you're going in."

"Oh my God. You're going to drop me." She wiggles, trying to get away, but I'm not having it.

I hold her tighter and laugh as I step outside, heading toward the water. "You weigh nothing. I'm not dropping you, and I'm certainly not letting you go." I walk quickly across the sand, which feels like hot coals, burning the bottoms of my bare feet with each step.

Bianca lifts her face toward the sky, eyes closed, soaking in the sunshine. "The sun feels so good."

"It would feel great on the rest of your body too." I smirk, wishing she were more comfortable with her body. I love the fuck out of it, and I haven't even seen everything.

"That's easy for you to say." She presses her fingertips into one of my pecs as she relaxes in my arms. "You're all hard muscle. Your body is perfection."

"Hard muscles or not, we all have perfect bodies."

"Bullshit," she mumbles.

The waves crash over my feet, finally putting out the flames. "No more body shaming." I lean forward, still holding her tightly against my body. "I'd spend hours worshiping your flesh."

She swallows hard. "Hours?"

"Hours."

"Guys always talk a good game. Delivery is another matter."

"What kind of men have you been with, baby?"

She wiggles again, and I relax my hold, letting her slide down my body. "I don't want to talk about the past right now."

Fair enough. The last thing I want to do is talk about the line of women I've been through before this moment. Though, I am curious what has her in knots and swearing off cock for so many months. Something must've happened, but she never wants to talk about it.

She's still clutching the top of the towel, hiding what's underneath, and staring up at me. "Where's your suit?"

I glance down and tuck my fingers into my waistband. "I'm not wearing one. Do you mind?"

"You weren't kidding about skinny-dipping."

"I never joke when it comes to being naked or having sex."

"Fine," she says with a smile. "Let me see, then." Her eyes go to my shorts.

"If I lose my shorts, you lose the towel." Somehow, the exchange isn't even, but I don't care. I've never been shy about my body, and I know for a fact that Bianca likes what she's seen so far.

"Works for me." She smirks. "I'm getting the better deal. Just so you know."

"I disagree." I pull at the waistband, yanking my shorts down my legs and kicking them to the side. I rest my hands on my waist, giving her an unobstructed view of every inch of my body. I motion toward her towel, practically salivating to get a look at her caramel skin. "A deal is a deal."

Her fingers let go of the towel edge, and the fabric falls to her feet in the sand.

I soak her in. Dark skin, white one-piece suit with only a small patch of cloth running down the middle of her stomach connecting the top and the bottom. Her breasts glisten in the sun, calling my name and wanting my attention.

"You're stunning." I take a step forward and lift my hand to her face. "You okay?" I ask because I know this was a big moment for her.

She nods. "I am. You didn't run away screaming when you saw my body."

I bring my lips to hers. "I'm going to worship you before we leave this island, Bianca. Every inch of you."

Her eyes sparkle with glints of honey in the overhead sunlight. "For hours?" She lifts an eyebrow.

"Until you're begging for me to stop," I whisper against her lips before kissing her.

She melts into me, pressing her breasts against my warm skin, making it impossible for me not to get a boner.

"I guess you like me," she murmurs.

My cock twitches, answering for me as I kiss her again.

Tonight, I'm going to show Bianca just how much I like her.

CHAPTER 21
BIANCA

"YOU'VE SPOILED ME," I say as I lift the champagne flute to my lips.

Vinnie rolls onto his side, propping his head on his palm. "You deserve this and more."

I stare at him in the dim lighting of the fire he made in the sand as we lie on the beach on a soft, large blanket. He served me dinner oceanside, and he cooked the meal himself. It wasn't frozen food or takeout, but he actually cooked me an entire meal from scratch.

"You're not what I expected."

The man is full of surprises.

He moves his body closer. "What were you expecting?"

The warm ocean breeze feels almost hot as it rolls across my bare shoulders. "Maybe some frozen pizza, but you're actually quite romantic."

"Don't tell anyone." He lets out a small laugh.

"You're good book boyfriend material."

He looks at me funny. "What's a book boyfriend?"

I chuckle. "The dreamy guys I write about that make readers swoon."

He gives me the biggest smile. "So, you're saying I'm dreamy?"

I nod.

He quirks an eyebrow as he runs the tip of his finger over the top of my hand. "Are you swooning too?"

"Maybe."

Who am I kidding? I'm completely swooning over this guy. Who wouldn't? He takes me away from the stress of the city to a private island where he prepares me dinner, not letting me lift a finger.

Vinnie moves my champagne glass off the blanket and inches closer. Our bodies are almost touching, and my heart's pounding uncontrollably in my chest. He rests his hand on my hip with nothing but my flimsy sundress separating our flesh.

"I'm going to kiss you," he says.

I see the fire and desire in the way he looks at me. I feel beautiful with how his eyes burn as they linger on my face. The air around us seems to crackle like the fire only a few feet away.

He leans forward, pressing his lips to mine. The softness of his mouth and the hardness of his body send goose bumps bursting across my flesh. His hand leaves my hip, sliding up my body and finding my face. There's something about having his giant hand holding my cheek and his thumb grazing the edge of my mouth as he deepens the kiss that sends my body into overdrive.

I roll onto my back and Vinnie follows, climbing on top of me and resting his lower body between my legs. My pussy aches to be filled after so many months.

He swipes his tongue over my lips, and I open to him, wanting and needing to taste him. His hard length presses against my clit, reminding me of the first time he got me off. He slowly pulls the strap of my sundress off one shoulder, and his fingertips make sparks burst across my skin.

I want to beg him to hurry because I've waited long enough to be touched this way. But I also want to savor every moment, every kiss, every caress, and memorize the way he makes me feel.

His lips blaze a trail down my jaw to my neck, nibbling and kissing his way to my bare shoulder. My fingernails dig into his biceps as I arch my back off the blanket, pushing myself toward him.

He pulls the strap farther down my arm, exposing my breast to the ocean breeze. My nipples immediately pebble and are in need of some serious attention.

I slide my hands to his neck as he moves his face closer to my breast. I want this. I want him. I want his mouth everywhere, sliding across my skin.

"You want me to take my time?" he whispers against my chest, glancing up at me.

I shake my head. "No. I need you inside me. I want you inside me," I correct.

He brings his mouth down over my breast, and he

closes his lips around my nipple. I nearly come immediately since my sensitive breasts have been neglected for so long and due to the fact that he's grinding his cock into me in the most delicious way.

I slide my hands down his chest, finding his shorts. I tug at the sides, wanting to feel his hardness against my body without anything separating us. He grunts as my fingernail scrapes against his skin, working the shorts down his thighs.

I palm his cock as he holds himself up with just enough room for me to fit my arm between us. The harder he sucks my nipple, the faster I stroke his length.

He slides his mouth across my body, and he uses his teeth to push the dress to the side, exposing my other breast. I stroke harder, working his cock, paying special attention to the tip and making it impossible to draw this out any longer.

I don't need flowers and courting. At this point, I'm a sure thing. There's a deep throb between my legs that can only be quenched by being filled by his hard cock.

"Fuck me," I moan.

Vinnie raises his eyes to mine, nipple still in his lips.

"Fuck me hard."

Vinnie sits up, cock pointing straight up toward the heavens, and removes his shorts. I grab the hem of my dress and wiggle until it's over my head, lying somewhere in the sand with his shorts.

"Are you sure?" he asks in the near-darkness as the moon shines behind him.

I prop myself up on my elbows and stare at his

beautiful and very naked body. "What didn't you understand about 'fuck me'?"

A smile spreads across his face. "I love when you say that."

"Fuck me," I say again because I'm going to keep saying it until he finally does what he's told.

I slide one hand down my stomach, finding my clit with my fingertips. I drop my head back, spreading my legs so he can watch me.

"If you don't, I'll do it," I tell him, dipping my fingers in my wetness.

He grabs my hand and moves it to the side as he shifts back between my legs. He slides a hand underneath me as one hand grips my ass and the other strokes his cock.

"I should get a condom," he says, but I'm too horny and, fuck, who has time for that now?

I glare at him because if I have to wait any longer, I'm going to lose my ever-loving mind. "Forget the condom. I'm clean and protected. Are you?"

"Tested monthly. I'm clean, baby."

I raise an eyebrow. "Then why are you still talking?"

Vinnie's lips are back on mine as the tip of his cock presses against my opening. "I'm done talking, baby. It's time to take what's mine."

I'd be lying if I didn't admit his words send goose bumps scattering across my skin. I write about men claiming women as their own all the time, but I have never had a man say the words to me. Vinnie knows just what to say to steal my breath and make not falling for him damn near impossible.

He slides his cock inside me inch by inch, stretching me so wide, I can barely breathe. The delicious bite as he pushes deeper has me gasping for air and clawing at his back. I moan his name as he pulls back and rocks back into me.

It's slow and sensual. He stares down at me, never breaking eye contact as his slow rocking turns into sharp, deep thrusts.

"Yes!" I chant over and over again. "More."

I hook my ankle around his ass, wanting him deeper, needing the friction for the orgasm that's slowly building inside me. His cock fills me, reminding me of exactly how wonderful it feels to be stuffed.

His lips are back on mine as he swivels his hips and grinds against me, hitting every spot I need touched to make the orgasm build faster.

My body tightens with each thrust, and I curl my toes as my back arches. I can't stop the orgasm. I scream his name, chanting into the darkness as colors explode behind my eyes.

"Again," he says, not stopping or slowing, but fucking me harder and deeper than before.

"I don't think I can," I say while trying to catch my breath, and tiny but violent aftershocks rock me to my core.

"You will, baby. I can do this all night," he says, and I believe he can and will.

CHAPTER 22
VINNIE

"ABSOLUTELY NOT," she says, shaking her head and taking a step back. "I'm not getting on that."

For a girl with a big attitude, she's scared of everything. I've quickly learned she's a creature of habit and never really steps outside her comfort zone.

"Just five minutes?" I try to grab her hand, but she snatches it away.

"Nope. Not happening."

I laugh as I stand where the waves crash over the sand and splash up my legs. "It'll be fun. Don't you trust me?"

"Obviously not." She laughs softly and crosses her arms. "Not enough to put my life in danger."

My eyebrows furrow. "Is this deadly?" I motion toward the Jet Ski. "For real?"

She points at the Jet Ski like it's going to jump out of the water and bite her. "If I get hurt, then what? How far is the nearest hospital?"

I shrug. "I don't know."

"Where's the ambulance?" she asks, giving me a smug look.

"There isn't one."

"You go." She juts her chin toward the water. "I'll stay here and write."

"If you're not going, I'm not going." I figure she'll give in if I refuse to go. I mean, most people would.

"Fine," she says. "Whatever makes you happy."

I step forward. "What would make me happy is if you would put that fine ass of yours on that Jet Ski."

She turns her face toward the sun. "I like land under my feet."

While she isn't looking, I bend down and grab her around the knees and hoist her into the air. Her fists immediately come down against my back, repeatedly smacking me as she howls.

"You put me down, Vinnie Gallo."

"You're so scary when you're mad," I tease her, laughing as I stalk toward the house with her thrown over my shoulder.

"Where are you taking me?"

"If you're not going out on the water, then I'm going to have my way with you. Remember the worshiping thing?"

All the fight goes out of her as her body stills. "Yeah."

I slide my hand up her leg and grip her soft skin near her thigh, right at the edge of her cotton underwear. "I'm about to see just how many orgasms you can handle before you beg for me to stop."

"You talk a big game."

I swat her ass playfully. "Baby, I always deliver on my promises."

She slides down my body, staring at me like I'm full of shit, but I'm not. There's nothing I want more than to explore every inch of her flesh with my lips, tongue, fingers, and cock. No spot will be left untouched.

"Take off your suit," I tell her.

"Just get naked? Right here?"

"Baby..." I slide my hand across her cheek. "I've seen every inch of your body already. If you want me to worship you, I need you naked."

The sunlight streams in through the windows as she slowly lowers the straps of her swimsuit. Her eyes never leave me as I take in the beauty of her caramel skin, full breasts, and lush hips.

"You're so beautiful," I tell her, and I mean every fucking word. "So freaking hot."

She stops her hand just before her breasts are exposed. "Don't talk."

"Why?"

"You make me nervous."

I step forward and place my finger under her chin, forcing her to look at me. I need her not only to hear my words, but to feel them too. "Don't be nervous, baby. I love every inch of you. I've never been so attracted to another person in my life. I'm about to show you just how much I adore your body."

She stares at me, blinking but not moving. I take over, moving her hand away from the strap, and I use both hands to pull her bathing suit down her body, showing me everything I'm about to devour.

I bend forward and kiss her breast as I pull the swimsuit down her legs. "I'm going to make you come until you can't come anymore."

"I've never come more than twice."

I'm face-to-face with her again, itching to get busy. "Well, baby, I'm going for the world record in orgasms. You're coming until you're unconscious."

She sucks in a breath and looks at me incredulously. "You want me to black out?"

I smirk. "I want you to never forget who owns this body."

"Well, fuck."

"We'll do that too, but first…I feast."

CHAPTER 23
BIANCA

LIFE HAS a way of putting things into perspective. You're riding high one minute, and then the world slaps you in the face the next. It's like the universe's cosmic way of reminding you that happiness is fleeting and fickle, ready to be snatched away at a moment's notice.

We spent four glorious days soaking up the sunshine in the Caribbean and somehow didn't stay in bed the entire time. Vinnie delivered on everything he promised and more. The man is a skilled lover, but there's more to him once you start peeling back the layers.

He lifts my hand to his lips as we wait at the stoplight just a block away from our building. "I wish we could've stayed longer." He glances at me for a moment before the light turns green.

I sigh, feeling the same way. I love Chicago. It's always been my home. The loud sirens, endless traffic, and people moving around the city, dotting the sidewalks as they hurry to wherever they're going.

I push my head into the headrest, knowing these are the final moments of our intimate escape before reality comes crashing in again. "Maybe we can go back after your season is over."

Vinnie turns to me with a smile, his fingers now laced with mine. He gives my hand a small squeeze. "You're not done with me?"

I shake my head and laugh. "I guess I'm not."

He pulls into his parking spot in the underground garage, puts the car in park, and turns to me. "I don't know how to say what I'm going to say. It's like a foreign vocabulary and something I haven't done since high school."

"Okay." I draw out the word and stare at him with a confused look because he's not making a ton of sense.

"If I come off like a moron, cut me a little slack. You're a writer and have a way with words, but I'm an athlete, and I usually use my body to show what I mean."

His body spoke volumes to me on the little island somewhere in the middle of the Caribbean.

"You're doing just fine." I try to give him confidence.

My words aren't as eloquent as he thinks. I have editors who help me not sound like a complete idiot half the time.

He reaches across the center console and grabs my other hand and is now holding both of them. He looks at me with his green eyes, a soft and warm expression on his face as he takes a deep breath like he's preparing for something big. "I want you to be my girl, Bianca. I've danced around the topic and said you were mine in not so many words, but I want us to be a couple officially."

I turn my body to face him, my brown eyes to his green. I'm completely rocked by his statement. Ever since my abuela said Vinnie and I were meant to be together, he's said he agreed. But I figured he was full of shit and saying what he thought I needed to hear for me to go all the way.

The small bit I knew about Vinnie was that he was the quintessential athlete. A player on and off the field. Nowhere did I find any mention of him ever having a long-term girlfriend. He wasn't a womanizer per his reputation or based on the comments I found about him on social media and from my limited experience with him. He was unapologetically a lover of women and didn't make commitments before now.

My reply hangs in my throat as my stomach does this weird flip-flop thing I describe so often in my books but have never experienced myself. "You want to be exclusive?"

He nods and squeezes my hands gently. "I don't want to see anyone else, and I want you all to myself."

I'm speechless, and that's something I rarely experience. "You want to go steady?"

Even saying the words is ridiculous. I'm immediately thrown back to high school when the boy I had the biggest crush on finally asked me out. I didn't sleep with him first like I did Vinnie, and as with most high school boys, that had been his goal—not falling in love and living happily ever after.

Vinnie nods. "Well," he says and pauses as his cheeks turn pink, "I know I sound like an idiot, but I want you to be my girl. I want the world to know you're mine too."

I squirm in my seat, and the car suddenly feels small and warm. My heart's racing, and I'm ready to say yes because Vinnie Gallo has made the last few days feel like a fairy tale. But something stops me. My past always has a way of worming its way into anything good. "When was the last time you had a girlfriend?"

He glances upward and grimaces. "Four—" he shakes his head "—no, maybe five or six years ago. I don't know. I was in high school."

Vinnie's the first person I've ever slept with that I wasn't already in a committed relationship with. Every single one ended in disaster with my heart broken. Although I write romance and happy endings, I've never found one myself. With heartbreak after heartbreak, I started to give up on the possibility that I was destined to find love.

Six months ago, after an awful and very public breakup, I decided I would not only swear off sex, but men and relationships too. It wasn't hard since I rarely leave my place and never put myself in a situation where I'd be tempted into the bed of another man.

The constant ups and downs of relationships made it impossible for me to write. It's hard to write about a dreamy guy sweeping a woman off her feet, when in real life, someone's busy stomping on my heart and making me feel like the most insignificant human being.

"But now you think you're ready?"

He furrows his eyebrows, and I can see he's hurt by my question. "Damn, Bianca. I didn't ask without a lot of thought first."

"I'm sorry." I feel like an asshole and rightfully so. He's pouring his heart out to me, asking for me to be his girl, and I'm questioning him and his feelings.

"Everything is different with you. I'm not going to lie. I wasn't always the best when it came to women. Very rarely did I ever see someone twice."

"See" is his code for "sleep with." Men like Vinnie don't see people. They sleep with everybody, sowing those ridiculous oats and living the life of a playboy like it's their job to spread pleasure to as many females as humanly possible in a short amount of time.

"Why me? Why now?" I ask. I have verbal diarrhea and just can't understand why he's ready to become Steady Eddie at this point in time. He has a huge football career in front of him and could probably get any woman on the planet in his bed if he wanted.

"That is exactly why."

I narrow my eyes. "Come again?"

"Because you question everything. You're not like most women I know. They would've said yes without asking why or even giving it another thought. You're complicated, difficult, and argumentative. You don't care who I am or what fame I might have. I think you like me for me, and the things I can do with my cock and tongue are just a bonus."

I give him a smile. "I do like you and not because of your cock."

He's an expert lover. I can't deny that. It's like he's spent a lifetime studying the best ways to please me and understands my body like no man ever has before. There was no coaching him on where to touch me to give me an orgasm. He just knew.

"Then say you'll be my girl. Just you and me. No one else."

"If you break my heart—" I start to say, but he releases one of my hands and places his fingers against my lips.

"Don't say it. I won't break your heart, but don't break mine either."

"How would I do that?"

He slides his hand around to my neck as he holds me tightly, sweeping his thumb along my chin. "Listen, I didn't date anyone steady because I wanted to be a player. I had my heart broken once in high school, and after watching my parents have a complicated relationship most of my life, I promised myself I wouldn't go down the same path. I wanted to wait until I found someone I knew I could love. Someone who challenged me and didn't just bend over backward to give me whatever I wanted. You're not easy in any sense of the word."

I laugh. "I guess I'm not."

"Trust me, you're not." He smiles as he moves his

thumb closer to my mouth, grazing my bottom lip. "That's what I like most about you. You're not falling at my feet. I had to work my ass off just to spend time with you. You're special, Bianca. I want you to know how special you really are. You turned my head with that attitude, and my feelings for you are already running deep. It would gut me if I had to see you with another man. Just say you'll be my girl already. You know you want to say yes. Stop being so stubborn."

This is the time when I'd usually dig in my heels, trying to prove I'm not stubborn, while being the stubbornest of all. But I don't want to be that way with Vinnie. I like the thought of him being mine just as much as me being his. I can't lie or deny that fact.

"I'm just scared, Vinnie. If you broke my heart, I'm not sure I could write another book for a very long time. My whole world would implode."

"What happens off the field affects what happens on the field. When my life is out of sorts, it shows in my performance. I'm putting myself on the line asking you this just as much as you'd be putting yourself on the line if you say yes. Relationships are a two-way street, baby."

The last few weeks have been wonderful, minus Susan and her sourpuss attitude about my new book. Vinnie's given me something to look forward to each day, and if suddenly it were all to stop and he dropped out of my life, I would probably end up depressed and drowning my sorrows in the bottom of a half-gallon tub of ice cream.

"I want to be your girl," I whisper.

He moves closer, turning his ear toward me, but I can see his smile. "Say that again."

"I want to be your girl, Vinnie."

The words aren't even completely out of my mouth before his lips are on mine. When he kisses me, the world melts away. Everything that's happened before no longer matters.

Vinnie does that to me.

"Thank you," he murmurs against my lips before pulling away.

"For what?" My voice is airy, almost breathless after the short but hot kiss he just laid on me.

"For saying yes." He licks his lips, and my eyes follow. "For being mine."

I know he's not perfect, but this moment, sitting in his car and with the way he's looking at me, is absolute perfection.

"Can we just stay here?" I ask, not wanting to go back to the real world.

I have a hellish deadline, and although I did get some words written while we were gone, they were nowhere near enough.

"You have a book to finish, and I have a starting position to win."

"Adulting is overrated."

"We have a few more hours until I have to report to camp." He quirks an eyebrow. "I could use a workout. You game, baby?"

"Ugh. I don't feel like running on the treadmill."

He smirks. "I wasn't talking about going to the workout room."

I swallow hard, and the dull ache between my legs that always seems to be there when Vinnie's around deepens. "Oh." I bite my lip and push open the door. "You coming?" I swing out my legs, the cold concrete of the garage touching the bottom of my sandals.

He's out of the car before I've even stood upright. "I most definitely am and more than once too. Leave the bags. We'll get them later."

"Someone's in a hurry."

Vinnie places two fingers under my chin and snakes his other arm around my middle. "I'm in a hurry to bury myself inside you, but what I'm going to do with you is going to take time. Lots of time."

I grab his hand, extricating myself from his hold, and pull him toward the elevator. "Stop talking. You're wasting time. Put up or shut up, Mr. Gallo."

I'm so focused on the ecstasy I know is about to happen, I don't look anywhere else except straight toward the elevators. But when Vinnie stops, pulling me backward with his face pale, I know something's off.

"What's wrong?" My eyes follow his and my heart sinks, and the dreamy love clouds I was just riding high on disappear. "What the..."

The word WHORE is spray-painted in red across the hood of my car. My mouth hangs open as I walk around my car, seeing the same word on the back and sides.

I'm shaking with anger, unable to stop walking in

circles around my car when Vinnie reaches out and wraps his arms around me, stopping me. "We'll get it repainted. It's not that bad."

Not that bad? This is awful. In the grand scheme of things, sure, it's not that bad. I mean, it would be worse to be shot or, hell, get the shit get kicked out of me. But there's nothing nice about the rageful act bestowed on my car.

"Who would do this?" Tears form in my eyes.

"Maybe a psycho fan." He holds me tighter. "Breathe, Bianca. It'll be okay."

"Okay?" I motion toward the hood of my car and suddenly feel ill. "How is that okay?"

"I'll ask security to pull the footage, and I'll call my guy to get your car fixed. Until we know who did this and why, you're not to come down here alone."

I turn my head and gawk at him. "Excuse me? First, you have a guy?"

"My dad's friend. He specializes in cars, and he'll get the job done quick and without any press."

"Fine." I take a deep breath and focus on the next part of his statement that doesn't sit right with me. "I'm not allowed to come down to the garage alone?"

He tightens his arms around my middle as he places his mouth next to my ear. "I won't let anything happen to you. Your car won't be here for a few days anyway. Take a cab or call me or my family for a ride anywhere. Whoever did this is nutty as fuck, baby. Don't play games with your life."

My body stiffens in his embrace. "You think I'm in danger?"

I've heard about other authors having overzealous fans and stalkers, but I've been lucky and have never experienced anything even remotely close to this before now.

"Yes. Promise me you'll be careful and listen until we figure out what happened or who did this?"

I still don't like that he's telling me what to do, but my father or brothers would say the same thing. I've always been fiercely independent, and listening to authority has not always been my strong suit.

"I promise," I tell him, but I hate saying the words. I hate that I'm suddenly a prisoner in my own home and at the mercy of some unknown threat.

"I'll keep you safe, and we'll keep this out of the press. Let me handle everything."

Part of me wants to argue and tell him I'll handle everything. But for once, I don't want to go it alone. I want someone to lean on, and I finally have him.

For once, I give in.

CHAPTER 24
VINNIE

I WIPE AWAY the sweat from my face as I listen to the voicemail left by the doorman at our building. The team workout went longer than I had anticipated, and I couldn't wait to get back to the locker room to see if they'd found anything.

"Mr. Gallo, we were able to pull the footage from the garage. It's not as clear as we'd like, but it should help in finding the person responsible for the damage to Ms. Hernandez's car. I'm texting it to you now. Please let us know what else we can do to help."

"That's some scary shit right there," Clarence says as he sits on the bench next to me, untying his cleats.

I tap the screen, going to my messages before the voice mail ends. Anger builds inside me as the photo loads. I know the hair and facial profile immediately.

"Fuck," I hiss, clutching the phone so tightly, I'm surprised the glass doesn't shatter in my palm.

"You know them?" Clarence asks.

I look down at Clarence, my body shaking with anger as I turn the screen so he can see her too.

"Oh fuck. I told you that bitch was insane."

Tracie is on an entirely different level from anyone else I know. It's one thing to bother me, following me around like a puppy dog, but it takes a truly sick person to do what she did. Coming after me is bad, but going after my girl or her property is a level of insanity I can't deal with and won't accept.

"That's it. I'm done playing games. I don't care who she is. I won't allow this to go without consequences."

Clarence shakes his head. "I don't envy you, man. She's done some fucked-up shit while I've been here, but never anything like this."

I take a deep breath, trying to rein in my anger before I knock someone's lights out. "Either they handle it, or I want off the team."

"Don't do anything you'll regret."

I level Clarence with my glare. "Should I just wait around with my thumb up my ass for her to hurt Bianca? What if she'd done this to Marquita?"

"I don't know, man. I don't know."

"Maybe I'll see you tomorrow, but this shit is stopping now."

I don't wait for him to reply before I stalk toward the coach's office with the photo still on my screen.

"Gallo," he says before I'm more than two feet inside his office.

"Coach. We have to talk," I tell him as I clench my

fists at my sides, trying to center my almost uncontrollable anger. "I want to be traded."

His head snaps back. "What?"

"You heard me. Trade me. I'll go anywhere."

"Absolutely not." He shakes his head and walks toward me, waving his hands in the air like I'm off my rocker. "You're going to be the starter this season. We're building this entire team around you."

I shove my phone in his face with the photo of Tracie holding a can of spray paint as she fucks up Bianca's car. "Tracie's gone too far this time. You keep promising me she's going to be taken care of, but nothing has changed. She's worse now than she was before. I can't work like this. I *won't* work like this. I can't have Bianca's life in danger because Tracie's allowed to do whatever she wants." My voice is shaking as my anger over the entire situation builds. "Either trade me, or I'll quit."

"Now, son," he says as he places a hand on my shoulder. "Don't do anything hasty. We'll handle this."

"I've heard that bullshit promise before, Coach."

"Rudy!" he yells and peers over my shoulder.

"What's up?" Rudy, the defensive line coach, asks from the hallway.

"Tell Mr. Turner I want to see him immediately."

"I'm on it," Rudy replies before leaving us alone again.

Coach steps around me and closes the door. "Sit down. He'll be here in a few minutes. I just saw him down the hallway talking to the press."

I do as he says, but I'm not relaxed. I run my hands up and down my legs, trying to calm myself before I have a complete and utter meltdown, ruining any chance at a pro career with any team in the league. The coach sits down across from me, not saying anything, but busying himself with some papers.

Moments later, Mr. Turner walks in. "You wanted to see me?"

I close my eyes and take a deep breath, knowing this is a make-it-or-break-it moment. I've worked my entire life to get to this point. I worked my ass off with two-a-days, endless hours in the gym, and perfecting my skills to make it to the big leagues. Now I'm here, and I may very well have to throw it all away because they can't seem to control one woman.

"Close the door, please," Coach tells Mr. Turner. "We have a situation."

Mr. Turner closes the door and makes his way across the room with very heavy footsteps. He glances at me and back to the coach. "What happened?"

Coach dips his head in my direction. "Show him."

I lift my phone, and Turner takes it from my hand, studying the photo. "What's she doing?"

"She's spray-painting the word 'whore' on my girl-friend's car in our parking garage."

He opens his mouth to say something but closes it again.

Coach motions toward me as he leans back in his chair. "Gallo wants to be traded."

"Absolutely not," Turner says, suddenly finding his words. "I won't allow it."

"Then I quit," I say and stand quickly. "I can't allow Tracie to threaten my girl. As of this moment, I'm no longer with the team and will be pressing charges against her immediately."

"She's gone too far this time." Turner rubs his forehead and grimaces. "I'll send her away. She needs medical help, son. It's hard to love someone so much when they're this self-destructive, but she's my blood. I'll send her out of the country for treatment at a clinic in Switzerland. Don't quit. I beg you. You're the future of this organization."

"Sir, with all due respect, you've promised me she'd be taken care of before."

"She'll be on my private jet tomorrow. It's a one-year treatment program. She won't be a problem since she'll be halfway around the world. Just please don't leave the team."

I have to admit, but only to myself, I like that he's almost begging me to stay. The starting quarterback position is mine, which is a nice feeling, but only if Tracie is completely out of the picture.

"May I speak with Bianca first?"

Mr. Turner lets out a heavy sigh and nods. "Either way, Tracie will be gone immediately."

Knowing she'll be out of the country for at least a year lifts an invisible burden off my shoulders I didn't entirely realize was there. She's been making surprise appearances wherever I've been for so long now, I just learned to ignore her. But what happened today, to Bianca's car, has gone too far. It's one thing to mess with my life, but Tracie bringing her craziness to my home, Bianca's home, is too much for me to deal with.

———

Bianca's on the couch next to me with her mouth hanging open. "You did what?"

"I told them I quit." I run my thumb across the soft skin on the back of her arm.

She shakes her head. "Why would you do that?"

"I had to. I told them if they weren't going to deal with Tracie, I was done playing for their team."

She rocks backward after hearing me say the words a second time. "What did they say?"

"Mr. Turner said he'd have her on a plane tomorrow and out of the country for at least a year in some swanky treatment center in Switzerland."

She scoots closer until our knees are touching. "Did you tell them you still want your job, then?"

"I told them I'd have to talk it over with you first."

Her lips form a little O before she blows out a loud breath. "You'd quit for me?"

I nod.

It's insanity, I know, but it was the only thing that seemed to make sense. I can't have Bianca feeling threatened, and I need her to be okay with everything and how Tracie is going to be handled for me to move forward. For us to continue.

"You can't quit." She intertwines our fingers. "I love that you would for me, but I can't allow you to do that."

"So, you're okay with me staying as long as she's gone?"

"Vinnie, a little spray paint isn't enough to scare me away—or for you to quit the team."

I spend the next twenty minutes explaining all the messed-up things Tracie has done in a little less than twelve months. From her showing up at my family's hotel suite in Vegas with no clothing, right up until she spray-painted Bianca's car. Bianca sits there in stunned silence the entire time, soaking in the insanity that's been my life since the day Tracie decided I was her next target.

"Do you understand why I had to give them an ultimatum?"

Bianca climbs into my lap, and I grab on to her hips. "I do. It's kind of sexy that you'd give it all up for me, but it's not what I want." She places her hands on my chest, and her pussy presses against my cock in just the right way to give me an instant hard-on. "This is your dream. You've worked your entire life for this opportunity. You need to call them and tell them you're not leaving."

I dig my fingers into her hips as I move her lower half forward and back, rubbing our bodies together like the first time we were together. "I'll call them in the morning. I have more important things to attend to." I smirk and lean forward to kiss my girl. "They can wait. This can't."

Before she can argue with me, I cover her mouth with mine, sealing away her words and the entire day. Nothing else matters but the girl in my lap and the way she moans deep in the back of her throat as I sweep my tongue between her luscious lips.

CHAPTER 25
BIANCA

I WAKE before dawn and lie in bed, staring at Vinnie in the faint glow of the city lights that surround our building. His massive frame takes up more than half of the bed, but he's peaceful in his sleep. It's my moment to study the features of his face and the dips and ridges of his chiseled body without being distracted.

Ever since I met with Susan, I've been going through a million different scenarios, trying to figure out how to end my novel. Vinnie's actions tonight and his willingness to end his entire career for me was a huge gesture. One a hero would typically make in my novels for the love of his life.

I never thought I'd be so content again. Opening my heart to someone else, especially a playboy like Vinnie, isn't something I thought would be possible or smart. But here I am, lying next to this beautiful man, completely and totally falling for him.

I slide out of bed and tiptoe across the room, grabbing my clothes off the floor as I make my way to the door. Thankfully, Vinnie doesn't wake. My muse is speaking to me, and I want a few uninterrupted hours to hash out the final chapter of my novel before it's due to my editor, along with all the changes I still have to make.

The words are pouring out of me, and I'm so engrossed in the ending, I don't hear Vinnie wake or notice him standing in the kitchen, sipping a cup of coffee, until I turn around, going for another cup myself.

"Did I wake you?"

His lips move but I can't hear anything he's saying, and I realize I'm still wearing my noise-canceling headphones I use to block out the city noise. I remove them, placing them on the center island as Vinnie laughs behind his coffee mug.

"You didn't wake me. I have an early practice, and I have to talk with Coach and Mr. Turner before I take the field. I want to know Tracie is gone before I tell them yes."

I rake my gaze over his bare chest. "Is there ever a day you don't work out?"

He shakes his head and places his coffee cup on the counter. "I never miss a workout unless I'm on vacation." He reaches out and grabs me around the waist. "If I didn't, I would be sore after some of those moves from last night."

"You went above and beyond."

He nuzzles his face in my neck. "I'm just beginning,

baby. I have a whole lot of moves I've never even tried yet."

I melt against him as his teeth graze my neck. "I look forward to seeing what you still have up your sleeve."

I'm riding high, floating on cloud nine in the arms of a man I never would've imagined myself with. "You better go before we both get sidetracked."

I want to fall back into bed, spending hours exploring each other's bodies, but my novel and his team are waiting.

"What are you doing today?"

"I have lunch with my mother."

I'm not overly excited by the idea. While I love her, my mother's ideas about my future and my own are very different. She's still not sold on Vinnie, and the last time I talked with her, I wasn't either.

"You'll need a car," he says and reaches for his phone on the counter.

I grab his arm, stopping him from whatever call he is about to make. "I'll take a taxi."

His beautiful green eyes roam across my face. "You sure?"

Moving onto my tiptoes, I kiss him quickly and nod. "Entirely sure. I wouldn't have taken my car anyway. Parking is murder downtown."

He wraps his arms around my middle and presses my body flush against his. "What are you doing Sunday?"

"Working, probably."

"Come to dinner with me at my parents'."

"Again?"

I had fun the first time, although it was a bit overwhelming. They were so much more relaxed compared to my family.

"Yes, again. It's a Sunday tradition, and Ma already told me to bring you. It's a requirement, and unless you want Betty banging on your door, I'd advise you to come."

I laugh, picturing his mother with her red hair, pounding on my door. "I like your family."

"Well," he says, brushing the hair away from my face, "they like you too."

He moves in for a kiss, but I squeeze my lips together tightly because I haven't brushed my teeth and I've already consumed a half a pot of coffee.

"I'll call you later."

I nod, still holding my lips together, and smile.

He's gone a few minutes later, and I'm left with my words and my characters who are just at the point in the novel where they realize they can't live without each other.

The hours breeze by as page after page pours out of me. I'm so engrossed in the story, I almost forget about my mother. When the one-hour notification pops up on my screen, I tear off my headphones and run to the shower. The meal is already going to be trying, but if I show up late, she'll have a frown on her face and chide me like I'm a little girl again.

———

My mother looks down at the menu, sitting with the most perfect posture. "I had Uncle Mateo do a little digging," she says nonchalantly. "He found some interesting things."

I drop the menu on top of my bread plate, not giving a single fuck about the clatter as the silverware bounces underneath. "I never asked you to do a *little digging,* and I certainly don't care about the *interesting things* he found."

My mother's lips pinch together like she's sucking on something sour. "He's not the man for you, Bianca."

There's no man on the planet, besides a chosen few, who my mother would deem good enough for me. Not one of them interests me even a little bit. They're stuffed suits who snub their noses at my career. That's a hard limit for me. My words are my lifeline, keeping me sane and happy since I was a little girl making up fairy tales.

I lean back with my hands flat on the fancy ivory tablecloth, trying to keep my voice low and not draw the attention of those nearby. "It's not your call."

"You're still my daughter."

"I'm completely happy for the first time in a long time, and you're going to shit all over everything."

Her smile tightens, always wanting to put on a good face in case anyone else is watching. "Watch your language, young lady, and your tone."

I laugh, but there's nothing happy about the way I

sound. "I thought we were going to have a nice lunch. I guess you had other plans."

"His father is a felon and a mobster, Bianca. Is that the type of people you want to associate with?"

I narrow my eyes. "Do we really want to compare families?"

Although my mother likes to think we're a fine, upstanding family, we have some pretty shady people in our tree. She's no one to talk or make judgments about a man because of the sins of his father.

"If I recall, your father wasn't the most honorable citizen," I tell her, reminding her she doesn't come from the well-to-do side of the family like she claims.

"My father made dumb mistakes when he was young. He paid for his crimes and turned his life around."

"Imagine if Daddy didn't want to be with you because of your father's illustrious past. How would you feel?"

I refuse to allow her to punish Vinnie because of something his father did in his past. It's not fair. No matter how upset my mother is about our relationship, she has no say in my future.

"His parents didn't like me."

"So, you're into repeating the pattern? We're not very close to Daddy's side because his mother never accepted you, given your family's history."

My mother places her menu down in front of her and shoos away the waiter when he approaches. "There were other reasons I never got along with his side of the family."

"Is that how you want it to be with me? You want to push me away because I've fallen in love with someone you don't feel is good enough?"

"You've only known him for a short time. Don't be dramatic. He's not good for you or your career."

"He's perfect for me and my career, Mom. He understands the long hours I need to work. He doesn't whine about me not spending enough time with him. He's the first man I've ever been with who doesn't pressure me to put my work aside to spend time with him."

"You barely know each other."

"Neither did you and Daddy before you ran off and eloped. But wait, you were knocked up with Luis, weren't you?"

I know my words sting her. My mother has always tried to convince us that she became pregnant right after they married, but we always knew better. She liked to play the I-was-a-virgin-until-I-got-married card on us kids.

"He's a playboy, Bianca. You're just another notch on his bedpost. Everyone knows how athletes are. Don't be childish and naïve."

"I'm well aware of his past." I stand and push back my chair. "If you can't accept us as a couple or Vinnie as my other half, then we can't have lunch anymore. You either accept him or lose me."

I don't wait for her to answer before I stalk off. I'm going to let her stew on my words and whine to my father about my disrespectful behavior. He'll set her ass straight. He always does. She's too quick to overreact and try to get everyone to do what she wants without thinking of our happiness first.

I refuse to let her talk poorly about Vinnie or his family. I'm well versed in the Gallo family after a quick Google search. I won't let Vinnie pay for the sins of his father, a man I actually like and who has, indeed, changed.

I'm halfway down the block, weaving in and out of the people wandering on the sidewalk when I realize I told my mother I was falling in love with Vinnie.

I hadn't been entirely honest with myself before that moment. I told myself I liked him or we were probably just a fling. But when he asked me to be his girl, and after our time away, I knew there was no one else I wanted to be with.

The man was about to give up a huge professional football career for me. Who does that? Only him.

"Bianca." I hear my mother's voice above the chatter on the streets. "Stop!"

I turn, finding my mother running in her high heels, waving her hands in the air. I almost keep walking. I'm sure she's chasing me down, ready to twist the dagger in my heart a little deeper.

"Baby," she says, trying to catch her breath when she finally makes it to me. "Forgive me. I was wrong. You were right."

This may be the first time in my entire life that my mother has ever said those words. "About all of it?"

She nods. "It's wrong of me to judge him on his father's past or his own. I can see you're happy. Happier than I've seen you in a long time." She reaches out and cups my cheeks in her hands. "All I want is for you to be happy."

"I am happy, Mom. Vinnie isn't who you think he is. He's kind, caring, selfless. He's everything I've ever wanted in a partner."

Her eyes water, but she shakes away her tears. "Come back to the restaurant and tell me about him."

I almost say no, worried it's a trap, but I know this is my one shot to explain everything to my mother and get her to back off for good. "Fine, but you're not allowed to say anything negative."

She takes a deep breath and exhales slowly. "I promise I'll listen with an open mind. Please, baby. You're my only daughter, and I want to know what's happening in your life."

"Okay, Mom. I'll go back with you, but if you say something again, I'm done."

She nods. "Okay. I can't imagine you not being in my life, sweetheart. If you love him, I love him. The last thing I want is for our relationship to be strained like your father's was with his parents."

"That'll be entirely up to you."

She grabs my hand, lacing our fingers together. "Let's start over. Tell me about your trip," she says as we walk back toward the restaurant.

I spend the next two hours telling her all about the real Vinnie Gallo. How he almost gave up his career for me, how he whisked me away to a private island to help me through the stress of finishing my current work in progress. I tell her everything... Well, not about the sex. There are some things that aren't meant to be shared, especially with my mother.

CHAPTER 26
VINNIE

I CAN'T WIPE the stupid smile off my face as Bianca strolls through the front doors of the training facility. The security guard gives her a quick chin nod as she flashes the pass I gave her.

Her eyes are on me as her high heels click against the linoleum, picking up speed the closer she gets to me. "I'm here. I'm here. What happened?"

I slide my arm around her back and haul her against me. "I got the job, baby."

She stares up at me with those perfect dark eyebrows drawn downward in the middle. "I thought you had the job."

I shake my head. "No. I got the starting QB position. It's a lock unless I fuck up during the preseason games or get hurt."

Her hands cover my mouth. "Don't say that out loud, Vinnie. You're going to give yourself bad juju."

"Baby." I tighten my arm around her back and grab

her chin with my other. "I'm too fucking lucky to have bad juju. I was born lucky."

"Well," she says with a smile, "you did find me."

"And got you too. Made you mine."

She nods. "That was pretty lucky."

I lean forward, holding her face up, and kiss her lips. The lips I now own. "See. I'm the luckiest son of a bitch in the world."

She slides her arm around my shoulder and digs her fingers into my hair. "Baby," she says, just like I do when I'm talking to her. "Maybe if you're good, we'll celebrate tonight, and you'll get lucky again."

My mind goes to all the dirty ways she can make this day even better. "Don't write checks with those lips you're not willing to cash."

The crease between her eyebrows is back and deeper. "Excuse me?"

I run my finger across her lush bottom lip. "I want to role-play."

"Role-play?"

I nod. "I want to act out a scene from your book. Live inside that pretty little head of yours for a while."

"You want to act out my book?"

I smile and squeeze her ass. "Not just any book. *The book.*"

"Which one?"

"*His.*"

She widens her eyes. "That one's so…"

"Dirty and hot as fuck?" My cock stirs in my shorts because that book was beyond anything my fucked-up and very perverted mind ever could've dreamed up.

She pokes her tongue out and sweeps it across her bottom lip, grazing my fingertip. It takes everything in me not to haul her ass into some abandoned closet and have my way with her.

"Well, it's been a while since I wrote that book. I don't know if I remember it well enough to role-play."

"Baby..." I smile and squeeze her ass roughly. "I have that shit memorized. We're solid."

Bianca glances over my shoulder. "That fucking bitch," she whispers and stiffens in my arms.

I turn my head, still holding my girl, and follow her eyes. Tracie's striding down the hallway and coming our way. "She's heading to the airport. Don't pay her any attention."

Bianca slides her hands down my arms before pushing against my chest and wiggling free from my hold. "I will cut the bitch."

I've never seen Bianca mad and never heard her ready to throw down. I like this side of her. I like it a lot.

I grab her arm before she gets too far away. "Don't, baby. She's on her way out. She's no one."

Bianca narrows her eyes, and her stare turns icy cold. "That bitch," she snaps and glares at my hand, "wrecked my car and called me a whore. That shit doesn't go down without me having a few words."

Where did this Bianca come from? The one I know, besides the minx who writes dirty-as-fuck words, is sometimes aggressive but never like this.

"So, you'd better get your hand off me and let me say my piece."

"Just be careful." I pull my hand away because this Bianca is a little scary.

I know enough not to fuck with a pissed-off woman. Daphne taught me that much. Hell, so did my mother. There are no two scarier people on the planet than them when there's hell to pay. Now I can add Bianca to that list.

Tracie's eyes are on Bianca as they march toward each other. I'm not far behind. If I have to, I'll throw myself in the middle because there's no way I'm letting my girl get hurt.

"You better wipe that smile off your face," Bianca says to Tracie when they're only a few feet apart.

Tracie laughs and comes to a stop in front of Bianca. "I may be leaving, but I'll be back. We both know who he belongs to, whore."

The bitch is clearly very delusional. I don't know if there's enough time in my life for her to get her shit sorted, no matter how fancy the clinic in Europe is. Sometimes crazy can't be fixed.

Bianca's entire posture changes, and I know what's about to happen. I've seen it before. Been witness to so many girl-fights. This isn't the first time women have fought over me, but this is the first time a girl I love is about to lay out another girl.

I reach for Bianca. I'm not worried about Tracie or my job, but for my girl's safety, because sometimes sheer madness overrules power and sanity. I'm too late, though.

Tracie's head snaps to the side as Bianca's palm smashes into Tracie's cheek. The crack echoes throughout the hallway.

Bianca steps forward, getting right in Tracie's face. "He's fucking mine, bitch. You come near me or mine again, and I'll end you."

I act fast, hauling Bianca backward and behind my back.

"Is there a problem?" Coach Malik says as he sticks his head out of the doorway of his office. His eyes move from me and Bianca to Tracie.

Tracie's holding her face and staring at us like there'll be hell to pay. "No problem at all, Malik," Tracie says in an eerily calm voice. "I was just leaving."

"Fucking right, you were," Bianca whispers behind me.

"All good, sir." I smile, but fuck, I'm so wound up right now, I'm liable to snap.

Malik doesn't leave, though; he keeps his eyes trained on us as Tracie walks by me. I turn my body, protecting Bianca from whatever Tracie's cooking up in that nutty brain of hers.

Tracie hums to herself as she saunters down the hallway like nothing happened. My eyes are on her, and so are Coach Malik's and Bianca's until Tracie pushes the door open and leaves the building.

I pull Bianca in front of me and grab her by the shoulders. "Where did that come from?"

She shrugs. "We all have a breaking point."

"I just never knew you had it in you."

"I'm sorry. I couldn't stop myself."

I wrap my arms around her and press her face into my chest. "Don't apologize. That was hot. You love me. You love me fierce, baby." I tangle my fingers in her hair, and I gently pull her head back to tip her eyes to me. "Don't do that shit again, though. I've never hit a woman, but if she would've hurt you, I would've had to deal with her."

"No, you wouldn't." There's defiance in her voice and the way she points her chin upward a little.

"You're my girl. It's what I do. No one hurts you."

Bianca laughs at me. "I'm not a delicate flower. I don't need protecting. My brothers taught me how to fight and stick up for myself."

"Now, you have me, and you don't need to handle your battles on your own. You're too important." I lift her fingers to my lips. "Your hands are too precious to be swinging them around."

She stares at me as I kiss her hand. Her lips are twisting like she wants to fight with me about this. I can see it in her eyes.

"Trust me to take care of you," I say before I crush my mouth to hers, stealing any fight left in her.

She melts into me, kissing me so passionately, some of it from anger and some from need. When I pull back, her eyes are still closed.

"Now, let's get out of here. We have plans."

"Plans?" She raises an eyebrow.

I press my hard cock into her stomach, holding her face in my hands. "Baby, don't play games with me. We've got a big night ahead of us."

"Big," she says and giggles.

"You're not going to be laughing later," I tell her. "You're going to be too busy sucking my cock while I play with that pretty, tight pussy of yours."

Her giggles fade away. "You really read that book?"

I tap my temple. "I have the fucker memorized. Be ready, baby. It's going to be a wild night."

EPILOGUE
VINNIE

One Month Later

"I THINK YOU'RE TOTALLY INSANE." Bianca fills a bowl with chips. "This is going to be a complete disaster."

"It's the only thing that makes sense," I tell her just as the front door opens.

"Hello," my mother calls out, her voice echoing through the mostly empty space because I haven't had time to finish furnishing my new place.

"In the kitchen!" I yell out.

Bianca grumbles under her breath as she pushes the bowl of chips next to the dip on the center of the kitchen island. "Don't say I didn't warn you."

The rest of my family is on the patio, waiting for my parents to arrive, and Bianca's family will get here in just a few minutes. We also invited her brothers, even though they still don't like the fact that I am dating their sister.

This is my one shot at turning the tide. Bianca told me what happened with her mother at lunch that day, and the last thing I want is for there to be anything standing in our way. I figured a party with both families was necessary for us to move forward. Either that, or the entire thing could blow up in my face and make the relationship even harder.

My mother rushes to Bianca and embraces her tightly, peppering her cheeks with kisses. "You look lovely, dear." Ma steps back, taking in the new sundress Bianca is wearing. "You two are going to make some amazing babies."

Bianca's face drains of color.

"Ma, lay off." I pull my ma away and hug her tightly while I mouth an apology to Bianca over my mother's shoulder.

"Always stunning." My father grabs Bianca's hand and kisses the back.

My mother doesn't last long in my arms because she's never one to stand still for more than a moment. "Where are my manners?" She tugs on the side of her dress and straightens the material, always trying to look so put-together. "What can I help with?"

"We have it all done." Bianca comes to stand next to me, but I snake my arm around her middle and haul her against me.

"Just have to put the steaks on. Bianca's family should be here any minute."

"I should've made coleslaw or something." Ma shakes her head. "I don't like coming empty-handed."

My mother's coleslaw looks and tastes like salad mixed with wallpaper paste. It's one of the simplest things to make, but somehow, she finds a way to make it inedible.

"Sweetheart." My father reaches for my mother's hand. "I think Vinnie and Bianca have it covered. How about a drink?"

"I could use a drink," Ma says, thankfully forgetting about helping us prepare the food.

"There's a full bar set up outside." I tick my head toward the patio and my brothers and sister who are outside drinking and laughing.

"Where are your parents, dear?" Ma asks Bianca.

"They'll be here any minute now." Bianca fidgets with a dish towel.

I grab her hand and pull her attention away from the rag. "It'll be fine, baby. Stop worrying so much."

"It's always scary when the families meet, but I promise we'll be on our best behavior." Ma smiles and glances toward me. "I'll make sure of it."

Bianca nods at my mother. "I know it will be fine."

"Give us a minute," I say to my parents, needing to have a quiet moment with my girl.

"We'll be outside." Pop pulls Ma toward the patio. "Take your time."

I grab Bianca by the shoulders and stare into her beautiful honey-brown eyes. "Take a deep breath."

She breathes in, listening to me for once.

"Breathe out."

She does.

"Relax, Bianca. Your family and my family will get along just fine."

"I don't know, Vinnie. This is a big step."

"It's a big step for both of us, but I have a secret weapon."

"You can't use your magical cock on everyone." She laughs.

"While that thought is both disturbing and funny, that's not what I'm talking about."

"How are you going to win them over?"

She always doubts me. I don't mind being underestimated. I have been my entire life. But the one thing I know is how to charm just about anyone. A trait I learned from watching my father.

"I got everyone season tickets to the home games this season."

"Even my family?"

I nod. "Everyone. I'll have my very own cheering section."

"That'll win the guys over, but my mom won't be too impressed."

She's right. I didn't think of that. My mom will love it because she's my mom, but Bianca's mother is a tougher nut to crack.

"I'll figure something out."

"I'm sure you will." She smirks. "You always seem to have your ways."

Bianca jumps as the doorbell chimes. "They're here," she says with dread in her voice.

"Just stand here and concentrate on breathing. I'll get the door."

I stalk toward the doorway, giving myself a little pep talk because I know this isn't going to be a walk in the park.

Her father's face is the first I see when I open the door. He's smiling and happy, but I've never seen another side of him. "Son," he says, and I like the way that word sounds coming out of his mouth. "It's nice to see you again."

"Mr. Hernandez." I hold out my hand and shake his waiting hand.

Mrs. Hernandez steps to the side, showing her beautiful face. "Vincent," she says, but this lady is in no way sold on me.

"Mrs. Hernandez, it's lovely to see you again." I take her hand and kiss the back, turning on the charm, but careful not to overdo it either.

"Likewise," she replies.

"Stop being so uptight, Luciana," Abuela says from the back. "Get the stick out of your ass and cut the man some slack."

I can't hold in my laughter at Abuela's words, but I glance downward so no one can see. Abuela pushes past her daughter and son-in-law and comes to stand in front of me.

"Let me see that face," she says, holding her hands in the air, waiting for me.

I give her my face, because I'd never argue with Abuela. "More handsome in the light," she says softly and brushes her thumbs over my cheeks. "There's so much happiness in your future."

"Abuela." Bianca grabs her grandmother and wraps her in a tight embrace. "I'm so happy you made it."

"I wouldn't miss today for anything, dear." Abuela smiles at her granddaughter like she's the greatest gift on earth.

I'm a little jealous of their relationship. I never knew my grandparents. All four of them had passed before I was born.

I back away from the doorway, motioning toward my place. "Come in. Come in."

Bianca lets go of her grandmother but is quickly swept up in the arms of her father. Mrs. Hernandez steps inside and looks around, taking in the mostly empty space.

"Gallo," Luis says as he steps through the doorway and gives me a chin lift.

"Luis, it's great to see you, man." I shake his hand, fully expecting him to squeeze my hand roughly to show his dominance, but he doesn't.

"I won't hurt you. At least not yet."

"That's nice of you." I laugh.

"Sup?" Javi says as he comes to stand next to his brother and me.

"Javi." I smile, but Luis's still got my hand in his.

"Listen, Gallo." Javi cracks his knuckles. "We like you as our quarterback, but dating our sister is another thing. And if you step over the line and make her cry, we're going to make you hurt."

I nod, knowing how it is between brothers and sisters. "I wouldn't expect anything less."

I'm not worried anyway. I'm pretty sure I can not only outrun them, but I could take any punch they'd throw my way, returning it harder and faster.

"Let's get you two a drink," I say when Luis finally releases his death grip on my fingers.

"Your place is nice," Mrs. Hernandez says as she plays with the pearls around her neck.

"I love what you did with Bianca's place. I was wondering…" I rub the back of my neck, hoping she'll take the bait. I think this is the perfect way to win over Mrs. H. "I was wondering if you'd help me decorate."

She looks shocked at my words. "You want me to decorate your loft?"

I nod. "I went to your website after Bianca told me you decorated her condo. I love your designs. I need some help getting this place in shape. Would you be willing to help me?"

"Of course." She smiles. "These lofts are a dream to design. All the light and open spaces."

"Smooth," Bianca whispers as she passes by me.

Right on cue, my father and mother come inside to greet Bianca's family. My mother's been excited for this day. My brothers' and sister's significant others didn't have much family, so this is a new experience for all of us.

"I'm Betty," my mother says before grabbing Bianca's mother and giving her a bear hug.

I laugh as Bianca watches in horror, waiting for her mother to lose her shit.

"God, you're so damn beautiful," Ma says.

Mrs. Hernandez eats up the compliment. "I love your hair, Betty. I'm Luciana, but my friends call me Ana."

"Ana, I'm so happy to finally meet you. I absolutely love your daughter. She's the best thing to ever happen to my son."

I'd have to agree. Even being picked in the first round of the draft doesn't seem to compare to the high I get when Bianca's around.

"Who's this handsome devil?" Ma asks, turning her attention to Bianca's father.

"I'm Jesús." He grabs her hand, kissing it in much the same way my father does when he's laying on the charm.

"Jesús." My mother repeats and gives the man a hug. "Your family is beautiful."

My father clears his throat because my mother's so excited and wrapped up in Bianca's family, she seems to have totally forgotten about him.

"Sorry. This is my husband, Santino."

"It's a pleasure, Mr. Hernandez." Pop smiles and reaches his hand out to Bianca's father.

"Jesús, please."

"Tino."

So far, so good. No one's thrown a punch or an insult.

"What fine-looking boys you have," Ma says, finally catching sight of Javi and Luis.

"Let's go outside," I say because this is getting weird and uncomfortable.

The love fest is great, but I need a drink, and by the look on Bianca's face, I'm pretty sure she needs one too.

———

Bianca stands next to me, watching our families talking nonstop. I hook my arm around her waist, pulling her against me as I look out over the city from the patio.

"It's going well," I tell her, feeling more nervous than I did when the day started. "Don't you want a drink?"

Dinner went better than expected. There hasn't been an awkward silence or a heated exchange of words. The siblings seemed to take to each other, chattering about sports. At their core, our families are the same. Macho men, bossy women, and filled with tons of love.

"No. I'm not in the mood. I need to keep my head clear. This has gone shockingly smooth," she says before taking a small sip of water. "Even my mother seems to be enjoying herself. Nice touch on the decorating bit too."

"I figured she'd like it and it would give us a chance to get to know each other better."

Bianca rests her head against my arm and sighs. "You're a smart cookie, Mr. Gallo."

"I'm always thinking ahead, baby."

My entire life, I've planned down to the smallest detail. High school sports and grades, the perfect college team, and my professional career. The only thing I hadn't planned was Bianca. I wasn't sure I'd ever find someone who would make me a one-woman man, but then she landed right in my arms like she was meant to be there forever.

"Are you happy?" I ask her, kissing the top of her head.

"More than I have been in a long time." She glances up at me as I pull away. "You make me happy."

"You don't regret breaking your no-sex promise to yourself?"

"It's a good thing I made that promise. What if I hadn't? I might have found someone else, and we wouldn't be standing here right now."

I hold her chin between my fingers. "You were meant to be here, Bianca. No man would've been right for you except me. We'd still be standing here, no matter what happened before the day I moved in."

"You're always so sure of yourself." She smiles.

"When I want something, I go after it, and I don't stop until I get what I want." I lean forward and press my lips to hers.

"You can be very persuasive," she says with a smirk.

"I think it's time for the surprise." I grab her hand, guiding her back toward our families.

"They're going to be so excited."

She has no idea just how excited everyone's going to be.

"Stay here. Let me go grab the tickets."

She nods and turns to her grandmother. "Are you doing okay, Abuela?"

I step inside, stopping for a minute to take in the two families and the girl who's quickly stolen my heart. My life is so full now. My days of partying are over. The playboy life I'd grown weary of has come to an end. For the first time in forever, I feel like an adult and totally focused on what I want, knowing exactly how to make it happen.

I take a deep breath and shake out my hands, something I've done before every big game I've ever played. This isn't a game, though. But there's so much on the line, and I could easily end up losing everything.

I grab the tickets from the drawer, along with the turquoise box I hid from Bianca. "It's now or never. I've got this," I tell myself.

Hiding the box underneath the tickets, I head back to the patio and my girl. She turns to me with a beautiful smile, figuring I'm about to make our families happy, but she has no idea the shit I have up my sleeve.

I clear my throat, and slowly the chatter at the table dies down as both families turn to face me. "Bianca and I want to thank everyone for coming today."

Bianca slides out of her chair and comes to stand at my side.

"I know we're all excited about the football season

that starts next week and Bianca's new book that'll be coming out in the spring. We wanted to celebrate our success with each of you, and I couldn't think of a better gift than season tickets for everyone."

I wave the tickets in the air before handing them off to Angelo who takes two and passes them on. Bianca's brothers and father are in shock as they stare down at their season ticket passes.

"They're for the family section," I tell them. "Open bar, food, everything's taken care of."

"Dude, this is huge," Luis says and isn't a dick.

It's progress.

"You didn't have to do this, son," Mr. Hernandez says to me, but I can tell he's happy.

Mrs. Hernandez isn't so impressed, but she puts on a good game face.

Bianca's beaming at my side. "They're happy," she says.

"One more thing," I say, taking her hand and placing the tiny box in her palm.

She stares down at the cardboard box wrapped in white ribbon. "What's this?"

"Open it," I tell her and push the box closer to her.

Her hands shake as she works at the ribbon, and I drop to my knee. The celebration of the family quickly ceases, and I know all eyes are on us.

Tears form in Bianca's eyes as she opens the box, and her gaze falls to me. "Vinnie, you can't—"

"Bianca," I interrupt and grab her hand as she stares down at the diamond ring. "I always thought I was happy, but I never knew true happiness until the day you walked into my life."

"Vinnie," she whispers, tears starting to stream down her cheeks.

"I know we've only known each other for a short time, but they say when you meet the person you're meant to spend a lifetime loving, you know it. I've never said these words to anyone except the people sitting behind me. I don't say them easily or without meaning them completely. I love you, Bianca. I want you to be my wife. Will you marry me?"

There's a collective gasp from the families as the last sentence leaves my mouth. Bianca's in tears as I grab her hand and take the ring from between her two fingers.

"It doesn't have to be now. We can get married next spring after the season's over, but I want everyone to know I'm yours and you're mine. I love you with every fiber of my being, baby. Say you'll be mine forever."

She hasn't said anything yet. Just cried. I'm about to panic and lose my shit. Maybe I was totally off base and she's more in love with my cock than me. We've never even said I love you to each other, but I know who I want, and it's her.

I'm holding the ring in front of her finger, waiting for a reply. Her mouth opens and closes, and I'm readying myself for the big denial I dreaded and knew could come.

"Yes. Oh my God, yes." She flings herself into my arms before I have a chance to slide the ring onto her finger. She kisses my cheeks and then my lips, mumbling, "Yes," over and over again.

I slide one arm around her, holding her tight, knowing I'm the luckiest son of a bitch in the world. "Your hand, baby. Give me your hand."

She holds out her hand, and it's still shaking as I slide the ring onto her finger. "I love you," I whisper.

"I love you too," she says with a small laugh before wiping away her tears. The sunlight splinters off the diamond, and she angles her hand away from her face, staring down at it.

"It's so big." Her eyes are wide, reminding me of the time I dropped my pants, letting her see all of me.

"Nothing but the best for my girl." I hold her face in my hands and stare into her honey-brown eyes. "I want to spend an eternity spoiling you and showing you how much you mean to me."

"Well, sweetheart," my mother says behind us. "We have another wedding to plan."

"Sweet baby Jesus," my father mutters.

The families congratulate each other on our engagement, and I even hear Mrs. Hernandez saying happy words.

I have my girl in my arms and my ring on her finger. What could be better than that? The day couldn't be more perfect.

Bianca grabs my face. "I have a surprise too," she says with a wicked smile.

"I love surprises, baby." I smile, hugging her tighter.

"We're pregnant."

"Are you kidding?" I whisper, barely able to find my voice.

"Nope. You knocked me up."

I'm going to be a dad.

A freaking dad.

My heart's pounding uncontrollably, and I start to feel sweat dotting my forehead. "I'm going to be a dad," I repeat, but this time out loud because it's kind of an unbelievable statement.

"You are." She nods with a nervous smile.

I lift her upward and twirl her in a circle, but the families haven't heard a word because they're too busy talking about our wedding.

"Don't tell anyone," I say in her ear. "Your father might kill me."

"It's our secret," she says to me, "because he will kill you or at least chase you around your place and probably get a punch in. Let's not forget my brothers, too."

When I place her on the ground, I can't stop myself from touching her stomach. "You're carrying my boy."

"Or girl."

"A baby," I whisper, still not believing this is really happening.

"I knew this day would come," Abuela says as she sits nearby with a satisfied smile on her face. "You better start planning the baby shower soon too."

Bianca's hand fists my shirt, and she stiffens as a hush falls across the table because everyone heard what Abuela said.

"What?" Her father's eyes narrow from the other

end of the table. He's not looking as happy as he did a minute ago.

"She's joking," Bianca says and touches her grandmother's hand. "Aren't you, Abuela?"

"Of course." Abuela pats her hand. "But a baby is soon to follow."

"Scared me for a minute," Mr. Hernandez says after his mother-in-law walks back her statement a little bit. "Not too soon, baby. You two have your careers to think about."

"Yes, Papa. I know."

I lean over, placing my mouth next to her ear. "How long are we going to lie to everyone?"

Bianca keeps a smile plastered on her face as our families go back to talking about the upcoming wedding. "Just a few months."

I can lie for a few months, right? I mean, it's not that hard to keep a secret this big from my family. Is it?

Thank you for reading. I hope you loved Vinnie and Bianca! The Gallo family saga continues is **LOVE!**

Angelo and Tilly are ready to say I do, but can they let go of their pasts and find true happiness? <u>Tap here to read LOVE now.</u>

DON'T MISS OUT!

Join my newsletter for exclusive content, special freebies, and so much more. Click here to get on the list or visit menofinked.com/news

Do you want to have your very own SIGNED paperbacks on your bookshelf? Now you can get them! Tap here to check out Chelle Bliss Romance or visit chelleblissromance.com and stock up on paperbacks, Inked gear, and other book worm merchandise!

Join over 10,000 readers on Facebook in Chelle Bliss Books private reader group and talk books and all things reading. Tap here to come be part of the family or visit facebook.com/groups/blisshangout

Want to be the first to know about upcoming sales and new releases? Follow me on Bookbub or visit bookbub. com/authors/chelle-bliss

LOVE SIGNED PAPERBACKS?

Visit *chelleblissromance.com* for signed paperbacks and book merchandise.

ABOUT THE AUTHOR

I'm a full-time writer, time-waster extraordinaire, social media addict, coffee fiend, and ex-history teacher. *To learn more about my books, please visit menofinked.com.*

Want to stay up-to-date on the newest Men of Inked release and more? Tap here to join my newsletter or visit *menofinked.com/inked-news*

Join over 10,000 readers on Facebook in Chelle Bliss Books private reader group and talk books and all things reading. Tap here to become part of the family or visit at *facebook.com/groups/blisshangout*

Tap here to see the Gallo Family Tree or visit *menofinked.com/gallo-family-tree*

Where to Follow Me:

- facebook.com/authorchellebliss1
- instagram.com/authorchellebliss
- bookbub.com/authors/chelle-bliss
- goodreads.com/chellebliss
- amazon.com/author/chellebliss
- tiktok.com/@chelleblissauthor
- x.com/ChelleBliss1
- pinterest.com/chellebliss10

Men of Inked
MYSTERY BOX

DELIVERED EVERY 4 MONTHS

SPECIAL EDITION PAPERBACKS &
EXCLUSIVE MERCHANDISE!

CHELLEBLISSROMANCE.COM

Visit chelleblissromance.com to learn more!

ACKNOWLEDGMENTS

I seriously suck at writing these. By the time I hit the end of a book, my mind is completely blank. It's like the vast darkness of space inside my head and it's a scary place to be sometimes...

To my readers and friends — Thank you. I can't even explain how thankful I am that you love the Gallos and the Men of Inked series. I will keep writing them as long as you'll keep reading. Thank you for taking some time out of your busy schedule to spend time with my family.

To the lovely members of the my Facebook group — Chelle Bliss Books - thank you for your excitement and uplifting words. Some days I'm in a funk, but you keep me going.

To my beta group - thanks for putting up with my insanity. I'm not easy, but you're always willing to read my words...for the most part.

To KA Linda for helping me through the blurb for this book. You're a rockstar and some days you're my much needed comic relief.

There are just so many people who help make a book come alive. To the betas, the editor, the proofreaders, and of course my crazy imagination. I won't bore you with the details, but I couldn't do it without the members of my team.

I'm one lucky son-of-a-bitch. If I had my ups and downs over the last three years, but I'm still going and the words are still flowing. Thank you for sticking it out with me.

More Gallos are coming. This is only the beginning...